Praise for bestselling author Joanna Wayne

"The shivers start building from the first chapters and don't stop rattling until the last climactic page."
—*RT Book Reviews* on *Son of a Gun*

"Wayne's got the start of a great series here as she slowly unfolds the events and characters surrounding an old murder while presenting a frightening modern mystery."
—*RT Book Reviews* on *Cowboy Swagger*

Praise for award-winning author Rita Herron

"Herron's still top of the line when it comes to bizarrely twisting plots as she piles up the obstacles to keep the suspense high."
—*RT Book Reviews* on *Cowboy to the Max*

"Herron gets it totally on target in this tale of family ties, insanity and death."
—*RT Book Reviews* on *Beneath the Badge* (Top Pick!)

Praise for reader favorite Mallory Kane

"Readers will almost taste the flavor of New Orleans in this mystery that's never about the whodunit but about the whydunit, all handled with Kane's deft hand at suspense."
—*RT Book Reviews* on *Death of a Beauty Queen*

"Kane creates feisty and independent women who are more than a match for their men, and this story is a terrifically complicated thriller."
—*RT Book Reviews* on *The Sharpshooter's Secret Son*

ABOUT THE AUTHORS

Joanna Wayne was born and raised in Shreveport, Louisiana, and received her undergraduate and graduate degrees from LSU-Shreveport. She moved to New Orleans in 1984, and it was there that she attended her first writing class and joined her first professional writing organization. Her debut novel, *Deep in the Bayou,* was published in 1994.

Now, dozens of published books later, Joanna has made a name for herself as being on the cutting edge of romantic suspense in both series and single-title novels. She has been on the Waldenbooks bestseller list for romance and has won many industry awards. She is also a popular speaker at writing organizations and local community functions and has taught creative writing at the University of New Orleans Metropolitan College.

Joanna currently resides in a small community forty miles north of Houston, Texas, with her husband. Though she still has many family and emotional ties to Louisiana, she loves living in the Lone Star State. You may write Joanna at P.O. Box 852, Montgomery, Texas 77356.

Rita Herron Award-winning author Rita Herron wrote her first book when she was twelve, but didn't think real people grew up to be writers. Now she writes so she doesn't have to get a *real* job. A former kindergarten teacher and workshop leader, she traded her storytelling to kids for writing romance, and now she writes romance comedies and romance suspense. She lives in Georgia with her own romance hero and three kids. She loves to hear from readers, so please write her at P.O. Box 921225, Norcross, GA 30092-1225, or visit her website, www.ritaherron.com.

Mallory Kane has two very good reasons for loving reading and writing. Her mother was a librarian, who taught her to love and respect books as a precious resource. Her father could hold listeners spellbound for hours with his stories. He was always her biggest fan.

She loves romance suspense with dangerous heroes and dauntless heroines, and enjoys tossing in a bit of her medical knowledge for an extra dose of intrigue. After twenty-five books published, Mallory is still amazed and thrilled that she actually gets to make up stories for a living.

Mallory lives in Tennessee with her computer-genius husband and three exceptionally intelligent cats. She enjoys hearing from readers. You can write her at mallory@mallorykane.com or via Harlequin Books.

JOANNA WAYNE

RITA HERRON

AND

MALLORY KANE

COVER ME

HARLEQUIN® INTRIGUE®

ISBN-13: 978-0-373-69674-1

COVER ME
Copyright © 2013 by Harlequin Books S.A.

The publisher acknowledges the copyright holders of the individual works as follows:

BAYOU PAYBACK
Copyright © 2013 by Jo Ann Vest

BAYOU JEOPARDY
Copyright © 2013 by Rita B. Herron

BAYOU JUSTICE
Copyright © 2013 by Rickey R. Mallory

PLEASE RECYCLE
THIS PRODUCT IS RECYCLABLE

Recycling programs for this product may not exist in your area.

This edition published by arrangement with Harlequin Books S.A.

For questions and comments about the quality of this book, please contact us at CustomerService@Harlequin.com.

® and TM are trademarks of Harlequin Enterprises Limited or its corporate affiliates. Trademarks indicated with ® are registered in the United States Patent and Trademark Office, the Canadian Trade Marks Office and in other countries.

Printed in U.S.A.

HARLEQUIN

www.Harlequin.com

CONTENTS

JOANNA WAYNE

BAYOU PAYBACK

CAST OF CHARACTERS

Remy Comeaux—Private detective and former NOPD narcotics detective with a grudge against the corrupt superintendent of police.

Nicole Smith—A beautiful survivor of Katrina who is currently dating Lee Barnaby.

Lee Barnaby—New Orleans Superintendent of Police.

Carlotta Worthington—Remy's fiancée before she lost her life in the flooding following Hurricane Katrina.

Charlie Gibbons—An NOPD detective whose partner was recently killed.

Doyle Shriver—An NOPD detective who was killed after suspecting someone in the department of corruption.

Sylvia Shriver—Wants to hire Remy to investigate her husband's death.

Mack Rivet—Former NOPD detective involved with the FBI investigation with Remy Comeaux and Ray Storm.

Ray Storm—An FBI agent involved in investigating corruption in the NOPD before Hurricane Katrina.

Dr. Cantrell—Nicole's employer.

To everyone who loves New Orleans—its culture, history, architecture, music, food and, most of all, the spirit of its inhabitants. And especially to those who lived through the devastation of Katrina and have helped in rebuilding the city they love. And a special nod to my Louisiana and Mississippi friends and family who truly know what it means to live in the path of Gulf hurricanes and their fury.

Chapter One

Remy Comeaux pulled up in front of the lavish Saint Charles Avenue mansion just before dark on Sunday evening. *Nice digs,* he thought as he took out his wallet and grabbed a few bills to tip the limo driver. Had he shown up in his beloved beat-up pickup truck, it might have been a little harder to crash the party. He wanted nothing to spoil the surprise he had planned for the guest of honor.

The last time he'd seen Lee Barnaby had been the day Katrina had roared into New Orleans, drowning Remy's hopes and dreams along with much of Crescent City. The night he'd lost Carlotta. His fiancée. His reason for living. His heart.

Lee had been only the deputy superintendent of police then. Not that most civilians or cops referred to him that way. In everyday matters, it was simply Chief or Deputy Chief. Tonight Barnaby was celebrating his rise to the top rung of the department. Remy was back in town to make sure his reign was short-lived.

Remy adjusted the uncomfortable silk cummerbund of his rented tux as he walked up the paved path toward the plantation-style home with its massive white pillars and wide verandas. Light spilled into the gathering twilight, and music and laughter drifted through the open doorway.

An aging, mustached butler stood sentinel at the heavy wood-and-etched-glass double doors. He scrutinized Remy for a few seconds, as if he were trying to place him. Evidently the limo and monkey suit were not enough to sell Remy as an invited guest.

"Good evening," Remy said. "Looks like I'm at the right place."

"Yes, sir. Can I have your name, sir?"

"Andre Comeaux," he said, using the first name of a cousin who just happened to be one of LSU's former legendary quarterbacks. "Just flew in from the West Coast. Wouldn't have missed this for the world."

"Yes, sir," the butler said, finally buying his act and flashing a welcoming smile. "Welcome to the Delacroix home."

"Thank you."

"Mrs. Delacroix requests that her guests gather in the ballroom at eight o'clock. Until then, the first floor of the house and the back gardens are at your disposal. Enjoy yourself."

"Thanks. I'm sure I will." Remy walked away as the next guests arrived and the butler went through his rehearsed spiel again.

It didn't take but a minute of wandering for Remy to realize that locating Lee Barnaby among the throng of guests in the sprawling house might not be as easy as he'd figured. A waiter passed with a tray of cocktails. Remy accepted a vodka martini. This was his first and no doubt his last foray into New Orleans old-money high society. He may as well partake of the perks.

He had to admit the house was impressive, though he couldn't imagine living here. Where would a man prop up his feet, pop a top and flick on the TV to watch a Saints game? Surely old man Delacroix had a man cave that was off-limits to Marilyn Delacroix's interior-design team.

Remy made the rounds from room to room, doing his best to remain inconspicuous as he scanned the partiers. He didn't come across Lee, but he recognized a few of the chief's pets from his old days with the department. The suck-ups who'd done Lee's bidding without question had no doubt moved right up the pay scale.

Amazingly, none of them recognized Remy, even though he practically ran into one of Lee's go-to cops from the pre-Katrina days. Charlie Gibbons had been the man who'd fastened the cuffs around his wrists the night Remy had been hauled off to jail.

Had he noticed Remy, he'd have no doubt raced to give Lee a heads-up that trouble was stalking the party scene. Fortunately, good old Charlie was far too engrossed in the cleavage of the woman draped across his shoulder to notice Remy.

Admittedly, Remy had changed a lot in eight years. He'd gained a few pounds—all muscle. Working out at a local gym and coaching a boxing team of underprivileged boys had become his grief-and-frustration outlet once he'd moved to Houston and started his own private detective agency.

He'd let the military haircut grow out. His nose, which had had been broken a couple of times playing football and again when he was a narc detective, had finally been straightened by an expert surgeon. And the boyish grin that Carlotta Worthington had loved had been replaced by a wary, brooding edge— or so he'd been told.

He stepped into a spacious dining room with rows of tall windows that offered views of a meticulously tended English garden lit by what appeared to be strings of stars strung through the spreading branches of dozens of century old live oak trees.

There were no chairs at the beautifully crafted antique mahogany dining table, but it and an equally impressive sideboard were laden with seafood. The oysters on the half shell looked too tasty to resist.

Remy had just slipped one between his lips when he felt a hand on his arm. He turned and looked into the deep violet eyes of one of the most stunning women he'd ever seen in his life, though she was likely twice his thirty-one years.

She smiled and moved her head just enough that her exquisite diamond earrings trapped the dazzling sparkles emanating from the multifaceted chandelier. "I'm Marilyn Delacroix. I don't believe we've met."

Remy smiled. "No, I don't believe we have. I'm an old friend of Lee's, but I don't get back to New Orleans often."

"You should make time. In spite of what you might hear, the city is almost as vibrant and lively as before."

"I can see that. And you throw a great party."

"Thank you. I didn't catch your name."

A young woman in a black suit without the requisite sequins and huge diamonds hugging her neck and dangling from her ears stepped next to Marilyn before he had time to lie.

"I hate to interrupt you," the woman said, her tone and manner all business. "Mr. Delacroix asked me to find you."

"Is there a problem?"

"Yes, ma'am. He said the mayor has been held up and he's not certain he can make it in time for the formalities."

"Oh, dear. We can't start without him. He's giving Lee's congratulatory speech."

Marilyn turned her eyes if not her attention back to Remy. "Perhaps we can talk later. In the meantime, enjoy yourself. I know you must be as proud of Lee as we are."

"Absolutely. He's a breed unto himself."

"My husband says it's about time Lee received recognition for all he's done for the city."

And Remy was here to see that Lee got exactly what was coming to him. The sins of old had ridden long enough. It was payback time.

By the time Remy reached the ballroom, it was teeming with guests. Couples rocked the dance floor to the beat of a loud, jarring tune Remy had never heard before and with any luck would never hear again.

He scanned the room, growing antsy when he still didn't spot Lee. Surely the guy wasn't late to a party given in his honor.

Finally the band took a break. Remy's ears enjoyed the moment until a woman's laughter caught him off guard, so hauntingly familiar it sliced into his heart.

He took a deep breath. His mind was playing cruel tricks on him. He had to get a grip. He'd known returning to New Orleans would bring back the old memories, but he couldn't let anything get in the way of what he'd come to do.

Yet when he heard the laughter again, he found himself walking toward the sound until he spotted the woman responsible for the free-spirited exuberance. She was facing away from him, but the straight, silky red hair that reached her shoulders was so much like Carlotta's that Remy had to struggle to breathe.

She was taller than Carlotta, or perhaps the height came from the silver heels that peeked from below a swirl of emerald-green silk. Her waist was as narrow as Carlotta's had been, her shapely hips well-defined.

Damn. Start falling prey to old desires and he'd make a fool of himself. Carlotta was dead. The woman with the lyrical laugh and burnished red hair was a stranger. Still, he was far too intrigued at this point to walk away without seeing her face.

He circled her and the young woman at her side, keeping his distance, but not so far away that he couldn't see the fullness of her red lips or the nose that turned up ever so slightly. Her smile was dazzling. Her features were striking. She was an absolute knockout.

She wasn't Carlotta.

He exhaled slowly, regaining a much-needed sense of equilibrium. But then their gazes met and for a second a sense of déjà vu ran so strong that it rocked his soul.

He turned away, exchanged his empty glass for a full one from the tray of a timely waiter and strode toward the double doors that led to the back loggia. He needed fresh air and to put some space between himself and the tantalizing redhead.

NICOLE SMITH'S GAZE followed the sexy stranger as he walked away. She was certain she'd never seen him before, yet for one brief moment, she'd felt as if she were drowning in the depths of his whiskey-colored eyes.

Her friend Deanie nudged her with her shoulder. "Who is that luscious creature and why haven't I met him before?"

"I've never seen him before, either, but he must be a friend of Lee's," Nicole answered. "Likely someone on the police force."

"May the force be with me."

"Your husband might object."

"Oh, yeah, him," Deanie teased. "But you're not married, and you're the one he was staring at. Go check him out."

"I'm here with Lee."

"Exactly."

Deanie made no secret of her negativity where Lee was concerned. She thought he was arrogant and chauvinistic, but it was only because she didn't know him the way Nicole did. Sure, he was tough. He was a cop who'd risen through the ranks. But he had his sensitive side, and he spoiled her in so many ways that she actually wished she were sexually attracted to him.

"Go say hello to the hot stranger," Deanie urged. "You know you want to."

"If I do, it's only because he looks vaguely familiar and I'm wondering if we've met before."

"That's as good an excuse as any to start up a conversation with a gorgeous hunk." Deanie put a hand to the small of Nicole's back and gave her a gentle shove in the stranger's direction.

"I'll go introduce myself if you go with me," Nicole said.

"You are such a wimp, Nicole. Besides, I'm going to find Billy. Suddenly I'm in the mood for a little romantic adventure of my own."

"If Marilyn catches you having a quickie in one of the upstairs bedrooms, you'll be blacklisted forever."

"I wouldn't dream of it. Too stuffy. I'm thinking about under the fake stars in the back of the Delacroixes' Saint Charles Avenue garden. How often does a lowly nurse get a chance to do that?"

Deanie sashayed off before Nicole could come up with an appropriate response. Deanie was bright, witty, daring, candid and totally unimpressed with money or social status.

The only reason she and her husband were here tonight was because Nicole had asked Lee to add them to the invitation list. Having Deanie around made these occasions a lot more fun for Nicole and she knew she couldn't duck out of this one, not when tonight was all about Lee.

Lee—her date for the evening, and yet here she was, drawn to a sexy stranger with mesmerizing eyes and a killer body.

Before she could talk herself out of it, she turned and joined him on the balcony.

Chapter Two

"It's a nice night for a party," Nicole murmured as she stopped next to the stranger.

When he turned to face her, a ridiculous zinging sensation danced along her nerve endings.

"A splendid night," he agreed. "And it just got a whole lot better."

A slow burn crept to her cheeks. Impulsively, she checked his ring finger. It was bare. "I love spring in New Orleans," she said, directing the subject back to the weather.

"So do I. But blink twice and it will have turned into the humid heat of summer."

"Ah, you know the city. Do you live here?" she asked.

"I used to—a lifetime ago."

Edginess crept into his voice, making him all the more intriguing.

"Are you a friend of Lee's?"

"You could say that."

"I'm sure he'll be glad you made the party."

"If I ever run into him. I'm beginning to think he dodged his own celebration."

"He's here somewhere," Nicole assured him, "probably surrounded by well-wishers or talking police business."

"No doubt."

She put out a hand. "I'm Nicole Smith. You look familiar. Have we met before?"

"No. If we had, I'm sure I'd remember."

His hand wrapped around her much smaller one and he held it. Her pulse quickened.

"I'm Andre," he said, smiling and meeting her gaze before finally letting go of her. "Hope you don't mind my saying so, but you do great things for that dress."

"Thank you."

"Do the Delacroixes always throw such lavish parties?"

"Always."

He looked around. "They have the perfect mansion for it."

"The gardens are lovely, too," Nicole said, "especially this time of the year. You should make time to see them."

His brows arched. "Is that an offer of a tour?"

"No.... I mean..." She swallowed back a twinge of guilt and a rush of blood that made her positively light-headed. "I would offer, but I have to get back to the party."

"That's a gracious brush-off." He leaned closer and slid his hand across the railing until their fingers touched.

Awareness sizzled.

"I should get back to the party myself, but it was nice meeting you, Nicole."

"Likewise," she murmured. She leaned on the railing and watched as he walked away, still reeling from the effect he'd had on her and faced with an undeniable truth.

Lee Barnaby had never excited her senses like that.

REMY WALKED BACK into the house determined to get his mind off the gorgeous redhead and back where it belonged. The woman had ignited so many sparks that he was still feeling the heat.

But he couldn't act on the attraction. She reminded him far too much of Carlotta, and not just her laugh. It was her hair, her eyes, her enchanting Southern drawl.

Even if he weren't about to jump into a blazing fire of his making, contacting her would be a mistake. And not fair to either of them, even if she were willing to see him again.

After another ten minutes of searching, Remy spotted Lee at the far end of the ballroom. He looked much the same as he had eight years ago, except that he'd put on a few pounds and his hair had started to gray a bit at the temples. Still, he looked younger than his age, which Remy knew was somewhere in the early fifties.

Remy cleared the few yards between them without Lee noticing him. He was seconds away from showing his face when Lee was joined by the seductive redhead.

Lee turned and slipped an arm around her shoulder, pulling her into the cluster of people who surrounded him.

The gesture and the smile she flashed for Lee appeared overly familiar, almost intimate. Remy felt a tightening in his gut. The woman had seemed far too nice to get romantically involved with a dirty rat like Lee—even if he hadn't been too old for her. Not that it was any of Remy's business.

Remy stayed out of sight, watching silently until Lee whispered something in the woman's ear that made her smile. Then the illustrious new NOPD chief turned and walked away.

Following quickly, Remy caught up with him just as he ducked into a small, hallway powder room.

Without breaking stride, Remy blocked the door with his foot before it could close completely. He pushed into the tiny room with Lee, then closed and locked the door behind them.

It was time to get reacquainted.

Chapter Three

"What the hell!"

"Hello, Lee. Nice to see you, too."

Lee's muscles flexed, and shock registered in every line of his ruddy face. "What the devil are you doing here, Comeaux?"

"Offering my congratulations. Isn't that what this celebration is all about?"

"This party is for invited guests. You're not one of them."

"I figured the engraved request for my presence got lost in the mail. But you do look surprised to see me."

"I am. I figured you'd crawled off and died somewhere like the gutter rat you are."

"No, I just moved on to a higher class of rodents."

Someone turned the doorknob from the outside.

"Out in a second," Remy called.

"Get out now," Lee muttered as the footsteps receded. "If you're still in town come morning, I'll have you arrested and thrown back in jail."

"Same old Barnaby. But threats and intimidation won't cut it this time. You're the one who's going down."

"Like hell I am. You're a criminal, Remy, a dirty cop who escaped from jail in the aftermath of a hurricane. No one will believe anything you say."

"No, but they'll believe the FBI and solid evidence."

"None of you have anything on me!"

Lee spit the words at him as if they were curses, but Remy could see the panic bleeding into his eyes. He'd accomplished what he'd come to do tonight—churn up enough anxiety inside Lee to put a serious damper on his moment of triumph.

The worst was yet to come.

"I guess we'll find out. See you around, Chief. Oh, and don't worry about the scintillating redhead. I'll see that she's well taken care of while you're behind bars and bonding with the guys you helped send to Angola."

Lee's face turned a violent red. Remy braced for a punch, but Lee merely called him a few choice names.

Remy had definitely pushed Lee's buttons with the mention of the redhead. The possibility that they were lovers galled Remy. He fought to stop it from spoiling the moment as he opened the bathroom door and left Lee to stew in his own well-deserved angst.

Lee had crossed enough lines of law and honor in his career to lock him away indefinitely. FBI agent Ray Storm, with the help of Remy and his former best friend, Detective Mack Rivet, had been close to proving Lee's guilt before Katrina had smashed Remy's world like a boot coming down on a rotten banana.

Before Katrina, Remy's participation in the operation had been professional. Now it was personal. This time he wouldn't quit until Lee Barnaby had a one-way pass to prison.

The only thing that would stop him would be moving into the Comeaux family mausoleum down in the bayou country where he'd grown up. Lee Barnaby was not beyond seeing that he made that move.

That was why Remy couldn't let down his guard for a second and why he had to work fast to gather the last shreds of proof. He wouldn't be satisfied with anything less than indisputable evidence that Lee was the most crooked cop to ever wear an NOPD badge.

NICOLE WATCHED FROM THE EDGE of the bandstand as Lee began his speech, thanking everyone for their enthusiasm and support and vowing to make the streets of New Orleans some of the safest of any big city in the nation.

Surprisingly, he seemed nervous, pausing frequently as if he'd lost the thought he wanted to convey. He wiped beads of perspiration from his brow more than once with a folded linen handkerchief, even though the room's temperature was comfortable.

It was a side of Lee she'd never seen before. Normally, he

reeked of confidence and charisma on occasions such as this. Something had clearly upset him.

In spite of her concern for Lee, she found herself scanning the crowd, searching for the stranger. She wondered if he'd had the chance to talk to Lee and regretted she hadn't asked his last name.

Not that it mattered. The rush of emotion she'd felt with him couldn't be trusted. At best it was a lustful burst of infatuation brought on by two glasses of champagne. She knew absolutely nothing about the man.

Lee quickly escaped the crush of well-wishers who surrounded him after the speech and made his way to her. Leaning close, his hand circled her waist and he put his mouth to her ear. "Let's take a walk in the garden. I need some fresh air."

"Are you feeling okay?"

"I'm great. I'd just like some alone time in the moonlight with my beautiful date."

Also not like Lee. He was thoughtful but never particularly romantic. And even as he led her away, he seemed distracted.

They crossed the veranda where she'd talked to Andre and then descended the wide steps to the maze of paths that meandered through watermelon-red azalea blooms, lush greenery and sparkling fountains.

Fake stars diminished the silvery glow of moonlight but didn't dim the serene beauty. But when Lee took her hand, his grip felt tense.

"You're not acting like a man who's just been showered with accolades," she said. "Is there something going on that I don't know about?"

"Just police business. Nothing to cause you worry." Lee grew silent and a second later dropped her hand and picked up his pace so that she almost had to run to keep up with his long stride.

They passed a couple who were so engrossed in each other that they barely wasted a glance on Lee and Nicole. Obviously, the garden's magic was not lost on them as it was on Lee.

Nicole's mind wandered back to the stranger. Her reaction to him was both disturbing and puzzling. It was if he'd tilted her world and loosed titillating sensations that had lain dormant for the past eight years.

Everyone in New Orleans had their own Katrina story. Nicole was no exception. But she was still alive, and like most of the others, she'd picked up the pieces and moved on.

But there were still the occasional moments when she experienced a yearning for what she'd lost, an ache so strong it consumed her. But never until this evening had she felt as sensually excited as she had with Andre.

That was surely a good sign, even if the feelings had been stirred by a man she'd likely never see again.

She was about to ask Lee if he'd talked to Andre, when Lee took her hand and tugged her to a stop in the dark shadows of a huge magnolia tree. The fragrance of the enchanting white blooms was intoxicating.

Lee's arms circled her waist and he pulled her closer. She looked up and met his gaze. There was an intensity in his stare that she'd never seen before.

"What is it, Lee?"

"You know how I feel about you, Nicole."

She swallowed hard, suddenly realizing why he seemed nervous and dreading what was coming next. She knew what he wanted from her. They'd talked all around the subject. It wasn't unreasonable. And yet...

"I don't think we should go there again tonight, Lee."

"I think we have to, Nicole. We've been friends for years. We've dated for months. It's time to move our relationship to the next level. I can't keep fighting my feelings for you."

"I realize that."

"You trust me, don't you?"

"Yes, of course I trust you, but I need more time, Lee. You said you understood."

"You've had eight years, Nicole. It's not time you need. It's just the courage to let someone into your life."

She knew Lee could be right. Even Deanie kept insisting that she let go of the past and open herself to the future.

"Move in with me, Nicole. Give me a chance to make you happy."

The proposition made her chest constrict until her breath seemed to be trapped inside her. "I can't make a decision like that on the spur of the moment."

"Then at least go home with me tonight, Nicole. I need you. I want you with me."

He put a thumb beneath her chin and tilted her face upward so that their lips were only inches apart. She stepped into the kiss, aching to feel a sensual onslaught that left her dizzy with passion. At this point she'd settle for even a hint of what she'd felt with Andre.

There was nothing.

"I can't. I'm sorry, Lee, but I can't."

His arms dropped to his sides and her rejection drew his lips into thin, tight lines. When he spoke, his words had a clipped, cutting edge to them. "If that's the way you want it, but you can't expect me to wait forever."

"I never asked that of you." She'd never asked anything of him.

He loosely linked his arm with hers. "I really should get back to the party now."

They walked in silence. Well-wishers gathered around Lee even before they climbed the steps to the veranda.

She left him to his admirers, called a taxi and went back to her condo. For all she knew, she'd just killed her relationship with Lee.

But when she crawled into bed alone, it was the stranger with the whiskey-colored eyes who tiptoed into her mind and stayed around for her dreams.

It was thirty minutes past midnight when Remy finally pushed away from the desk in his hotel room. He'd spent the past three hours staring at his findings, which never fully solved the puzzle of exactly how deep Lee Barnaby had been involved in the pre-Katrina police corruption. Weary, Remy stood, stretched and then walked to the window.

He'd chosen an old hotel on the outskirts of the French Quarter, not for its quaintness or its reasonable price but because he liked the way the pace here slowed to a skulking crawl.

The bars were not as noisy as the ones on Bourbon Street. The inhabitants were an eclectic mix of cultures, socioeconomic levels and gender preferences. He could easily go unnoticed here.

But it was another part of the city that called to him tonight. Remy headed to his truck and took the short drive to an area that had taken the brunt of the flooding when the levies were breached.

What-ifs tormented his mind as he drove the once-familiar streets, finally stopping in front of the hospital where Carlotta had worked as a nurse. She'd loved her job.

She'd loved life. She'd loved him. She'd teased him about being a cop, calling him her armed protector.

But when she'd needed him most, he hadn't been there. The memories returned full force and with them the crushing sense of loss that the passing years had barely dimmed.

But sinking back into the mire was the last thing he needed now. He turned the key in the ignition and brought the pickup truck's engine to life. He was about to pull into the street when a car with no lights on pulled up behind him and stopped, blocking his exit.

Instinctively, he braced for trouble and reached for the pistol he kept holstered beneath his seat. When he saw Charlie Gibbons behind the wheel, he knew his instincts were right on target.

Chapter Four

Charlie jumped out of his car and walked toward Remy, his hands in the open.

Remy lowered his window. "What's a nice suck-up cop like you doing in a place like this?"

"Following you."

"I didn't figure Barnaby would waste much time siccing one of his lapdogs on me."

"The chief didn't send me. I'm here on my own."

"And when I buy that, you'll sell me the Saint Louis Cathedral."

"I'm not asking you to buy anything, Remy. I'd just like to talk."

"Then shoot."

"How about somewhere more private than the middle of the street?"

"Where might that be?"

"There's a park a few blocks from here. It's likely deserted this time of night."

A dark, deserted park with no witnesses, the perfect spot to get rid of an annoying ex-cop. But the prospect of hearing Charlie out intrigued Remy. Remy would just have to watch his own back. He was used to that.

"Lead the way," Remy said. "I'll follow. But I'm warning you. If this is a trap, I shoot *you* first."

"Not strong on trust, are you?"

"Sure I am. I trust my Smith & Wesson."

A few minutes later, Remy followed him into a small asphalt lot next to a fenced playground. There was not another car or person in sight, but that didn't mean there wasn't someone hiding in the shadows or in the woods that bordered the far side of the park.

Charlie got out of his car and joined Remy in his, sliding into the passenger seat.

Remy moved his seat back and shifted so that he was facing him. "Now, do you want to tell me what this is about?"

"I know you were working with the FBI before Katrina on some secret task force."

"Apparently not secret enough."

"Word has a way of leaking into the mainstream. Was Lee Barnaby part of that investigation?"

"Lee must have thought so. Why else did he have you arrest me when he should have been focused on keeping his citizens safe during the approaching storm?"

"Maybe because he was convinced you were on the take."

"Sure I was. That's why the FBI invited me to the party. Don't mess with me, Charlie. You got something to say, say it straight."

"Okay. What do you have on Lee?"

"Give me one good reason why I should share that with the biggest butt kisser in the department."

Moments of silence seethed with tension before Charlie exhaled sharply and turned back to Remy. "My partner was killed while driving home from a crime scene three weeks ago. Someone just pulled up next to him at a red light and fired three bullets into his brain."

"Have you arrested the scum who did it?"

"We don't have the first lead, but I have reason to suspect that one of the higher-ups in the department may have put out a hit on him."

Remy studied Charlie's expression, looking for a sign that the bomb he'd just dropped was part of a setup. All he saw was a determined jut of the jaw and a grim expression that suggested Charlie just might be telling the truth. If he was and Lee was behind this, he'd moved a long way past taking bribes from drug dealers.

"Care to explain that?" Remy asked.

"My partner came to me two days before he was killed and said he was tired of putting his life on the line to arrest murderers only to have them walk without a trial."

"That's it? Cops say that all the time. If it's not the grand jury, it's some spineless judge who cuts them loose."

"Yes, but this time my partner said he'd been doing a little investigating on his own and that when he was through, the ax that fell would be chopping heads, starting at the top of the feeding chain."

"Did he name names?"

"No, he wouldn't say, but he told me that if anything happened to him to watch out for his wife. I think he suspected his personal investigation might get him killed."

"What was your partner's name?"

"Doyle Shriver. A great guy. Wife, two kids. Just promoted to homicide detective about six months ago. I don't want to believe Lee had anything to do with his murder," Charlie admitted. "But I can't ignore the possibility."

Remy shrugged. "Frankly, I wouldn't put anything past him."

"So what did the FBI have on Lee?" Charlie asked again.

Remy decided to level with him. He had a hunch he'd need a source on the inside before this was over. Charlie might turn out to be his man. Stranger things had happened.

"A group of dirty cops were taking payoffs to see that certain dealers were left alone while others were arrested and removed from the competition. The money trail led directly to Lee."

"Were those facts or suspicions?" Charlie asked.

"Facts."

"Why weren't there arrests?"

"They would have come eventually. But Lee Barnaby was only a small part of the FBI's investigation. The scope went far beyond the police department. Even I wasn't privy to their full investigation or findings."

"So why was the investigation dropped after Katrina?"

"By the time I got back to my apartment, it had been looted. All my files and my computer were long gone. I was back to square one. Then I was told by the FBI that my services would no longer be needed. At the time, I figured that my untimely arrest made me a less valuable addition to the team. But since no arrests were ever made, it appears the case was just dropped in the destructive aftermath of Katrina."

Charlie nodded. "Like so many other cases under investigation at the time."

"So where do you plan to go with your suspicions?" Remy asked.

"I'm not sure. But it seems I owe something to Doyle's wife and kids."

"Start asking questions and you may just get yourself killed," Remy warned him.

"Not if I can help it."

"How about just keeping a low profile for a few days?" Remy said. "Find out what you can without taking any real risks. In the meantime, I'm working a couple of angles that should firm up my case against Lee."

"I kind of figured that was why you were back in town and at the party tonight."

"So Lee told you about our encounter?"

"No. I saw you out on the balcony talking to Nicole Smith. What kind of encounter did you have with Lee?"

"I just let him know that I was taking him down."

Charlie emitted a low whistle. "That explains his mood when I ran into him as he was leaving. Looks like I'm not the only one who'd best watch their back every second."

"Yep. The heat is on. But this time I'm going to be the one stoking the fire." Unless a bullet got to him first. "By the way, what's the name of the guy Shriver arrested who got off without a trial?"

"Reggio Sanchez. Have you heard of him?"

"Know him well." In fact, Remy had arrested him on more than one occasion himself. Reggio had never gone to trial on any of those charges, either. Eyewitnesses against Reggio had a way of forgetting what they saw or else completely disappearing.

"What was the charge when he was arrested?"

"Murder."

"Who was the alleged victim?"

"Jessie Klein. She was an eyewitness in the murder of her son Rick. She claimed that she saw Reggio pull the trigger."

"Reggio used to be the meanest SOB this side of hell," Remy said."

"He still is," Charlie assured him.

"Then I won't expect him to offer me a beer when I come calling."

But that wouldn't be tonight. Remy needed sleep and time to think. Tying Lee to the murder of a cop would seal the deal. All he needed was proof positive that Lee had ordered the hit on one of his own officers.

He didn't have a clue how he was going to get that.

SILVERY BEAMS SHIMMERED on the waves that lapped the shoreline of Lake Ponchartrain. Nicole lifted her long hair from her neck and let the gentle breeze cool her skin.

She swayed against the man who held her other hand, the thrill of his touch searing through her.

"I could stay here forever," she whispered.

"I could stay anywhere forever as long as I'm with you."

She looked into his eyes as he pulled her closer. Excitement swelled to a crescendo as his lips lowered to hers.

She melted into the kiss as her body arched toward him, anticipation soaring. His kiss was ecstasy, but she wanted more, so much more. She wanted all of him, throbbing inside her, making them one.

They fell to the grass, a tangle of arms and legs and passion.

But then the water began to rush over the banks, washing over them, dragging them into the depths as it receded. She couldn't breathe.

She reached for her lover, but he wasn't there.

Nicole jerked awake. She sat up straight, shaking, the dregs of the dream refusing to let go of her. Cold sweat made her nightshirt cling to her body. She yanked it over her head and slung it across the room.

When her heart stopped pounding, she slid from her bed and padded barefoot to the window that overlooked the lighted walkway threading through the upscale town-house complex. She'd had various versions of this nightmare before, but this time it had been different. This time it was so real she could still feel the pressure of the kiss and the heat from the desire.

And this time, the man had not been just a shadowy, unidentifiable illusion. What was wrong with her that she found a virtual stranger so provocative and seductive that he'd invaded her thoughts and now her dreams?

Why was she so fascinated by him when every other man she'd met in years left her cold? This schoolgirl infatuation was beyond ridiculous. She should shake it before she made a complete fool of herself.

Yet deep inside she knew she had to find a way to see him again.

Chapter Five

Remy stepped out of the shower, water dripping from his body and soaking into the terry tub mat. He grabbed a towel from the rack and dried his thick hair with it before wrapping it around his waist.

His cell phone rang as he reached for his toothbrush. He rushed back to the bedside table, grabbed it and checked the caller ID. Sylvia Shriver. Same last name as Charlie's late partner. He quickly took the unexpected call.

"Remy Comeaux here."

"I'm Syl, Doyle Shriver's wife. I hope I didn't call you too early."

"Not at all. How can I help you?"

"Charlie Gibbons called me a few minutes ago. He told me he'd talked to you and that he might be closer to finding out who shot Doyle. But he cautioned me not to mention his seeing you to anyone."

There was a quake in her voice when she said her dead husband's name. Clearly, making this call wasn't easy for her.

"Charlie and I talked," Remy said, surprised that Charlie had told Sylvia about their meeting. "I'm not sure I said anything that would help."

"Perhaps he was just trying to reassure me. I cry every time I talk to him."

Maybe Remy had grown too cynical. Perhaps the guy did just have a heart.

"After I talked to Charlie, I looked you up on the internet," Syl said. "You have an impressive reputation. I'd like to hire you to help me find Doyle's killer."

"You have Charlie for that."

"I'm not sure that's enough. Do you think you could possibly find time to stop by my house this morning?"

"I'll make time."

"Just one other thing," she said. "If you talk to Charlie, please don't mention that I called. I'll explain when I see you."

He'd hold her to that. "I'll need an address."

She gave him that and the directions. He was ringing her door-bell in under a half hour.

An attractive woman with short blond hair and striking blue eyes ringed with the dark circles of tears and grief opened the door. A toddler clung to the hem of her white shorts.

"I'm Remy," he said.

"I'm Syl." She rested her hand on the boy's shoulder. "This is Toby."

"Good morning, Toby."

Toby hid his face behind his mother's leg as she motioned Remy inside.

"Could I get you some coffee?" she asked.

"Coffee would be great."

The toddler finally let go of her shorts and stood staring at Remy.

Syl took his hand. "Come with me, Toby. I bet Grandma has your Cheerios all ready for you."

Remy looked around. The room was cluttered with blocks and toy cars. A playpen that held colorful teething rings and a pacifier was set up in the corner. Apparently, the second child Charlie had mentioned was even younger than Toby.

Children who'd grow up without a father. The idea that Lee could be behind Doyle Shriver's death was so revolting it turned Remy's stomach.

Remy took a seat on the sofa and stared at the dozens of snap-shots strewn about the coffee table. The same man appeared in all of them, some with him in his NOPD uniform. Many were of him and Syl. Some included the kids. In all of them Doyle looked as if he were a man with everything to live for.

Remy imagined Syl going through the photos, trying to hold

on to them so tightly that she could will Doyle back to life. He understood the feeling of hopelessness far too well.

That didn't mean he had any idea what to say to her that might help. He hadn't wanted to face any of his friends for months after Carlotta's death.

"Milk or sugar?" Syl called from the kitchen.

"Just black."

She returned with two mugs and set them both on the coffee table in front of him.

"If you're considering taking the case, I have something you should see."

"You should realize going in that involving me might unleash an avalanche of complications."

"I don't care what it unleashes as long as there's justice for Doyle." She disappeared again, and when she came back, she handed him a manila folder.

"I found this two days ago when I finally forced myself to go through the file cabinet where my husband kept all our important papers."

The file was labeled Reggio Sanchez.

Remy opened it and examined the contents. There were scribbled notes, police reports and copies of pictures taken at a crime scene. He glanced at the pictures of an elderly woman in a baggy black coat who'd been shot in the head. From the damage, he'd guess she'd been shot several times at close range.

He removed a copy of an official police report signed by Doyle. The document stated that film taken from the hidden camera outside Klein's Café had shown Reggie Sanchez follow Jessie Klein through the back door of her restaurant when she showed up for work at 5:40 a.m. on the day of her murder.

Reggie Sanchez had left the restaurant alone ten minutes later. There was a stain that looked to be blood on the front of his shirt. The first employee on duty that morning had discovered Jessie Klein's body.

"Jessie Klein was the only eyewitness to the murder of her grandson," Syl explained. "Reggie Sanchez had pulled the trigger and killed him in front of his house in cold blood. Supposedly it involved a drug-deal double cross of some kind."

"If they had the film, why isn't Sanchez in jail for Jessie's murder?"

"The film came up missing from the evidence file just before the case was to go to a grand jury," Syl said. "And Sanchez came up with some kind of supposedly airtight alibi that Doyle was sure was fake. When Sanchez was released, Doyle was furious."

Syl looked down at the table of scattered snapshots and grew silent.

"I'm sure he was," Remy said, encouraging her to keep talking. "Did he have a theory on what happened to the film?"

"Not that he shared with me. But he was more upset than I'd ever seen him. He said he wouldn't stop until he found out who was responsible."

Her eyes filled with tears and her voice began to tremble. "I know finding the man responsible for his death won't bring Doyle back, but he deserves at least that much."

"I agree," Remy said.

"Does that mean you'll take the case?"

"No, at least not for money. But I'll look into it. Let's just consider this a favor from one ex-member of the NOPD to another."

"I appreciate that. I mean, I don't how I'm going to make ends meet as it is. But please don't tell Charlie that I've talked to you. I don't think Doyle fully trusted him in the end. So I don't trust him, either."

"You got it. I'll get back to you when I have something to report. In the meantime, you just take care of yourself and the boys. That's what your husband would want above all."

And if Lee had actually killed Doyle or ordered his assassination, there was no telling what extremes he'd go to to hide his guilt or who might be in danger.

An image of Lee with his arm around Nicole sprang to Remy's mind. Agitation steeled his nerves and ground in his gut. He couldn't bear the thought of her with him.

But even if he went to her and told her what he knew about

Lee, there wasn't a reason on earth why she'd believe him. He'd even lied to her about his name.

Remy spent the rest of the day trying to track down Reggio Sanchez. His search sent him to seedy areas of the city dominated by crack houses and half-deserted neighborhoods. It was easy to spot drug deals being carried out on street corners, frequently in the presence of kids riding by on their bikes or young mothers out walking with their children.

Much of the city had been rebuilt since the hurricane by citizens with determination and the help of warmhearted people from all across the country. But there were still pockets of destruction where abandoned schools, businesses and homes with broken windows and rotting structures served as havens for crime and criminals.

Remy had worked as a narcotics detective long enough that he knew the routine, but he'd also been away long enough that he'd lost most of his contacts. The squealers who remained knew he had no clout, so there was no real reason for them to confide in him.

By midafternoon Remy was hungry, frustrated and found it impossible to get Nicole off his mind. He drove to the Bucktown area and was pleasantly surprised to find that one of his favorite dives from the old days had been rebuilt.

He parked and went inside. It was smaller than before but still smelled of frying seafood, hot sauces and oven-fresh French bread. He ordered a dressed oyster po'boy and a cold beer from the counter and then chose a table in the back.

While he waited on the sandwich, he pulled out his laptop and started a search to see what he could dig up on Nicole Smith. Given a little time, on and off the computer, he could and frequently did uncover things about a person that even their spouses didn't know.

By the time the waitress set his cold beer in front of him, he knew Nicole's full name, her address, phone number and that she worked in the office of Dr. Rodney Cantrell.

By the time he'd finished the giant slabs of French bread,

stuffed to overflowing with crispy oysters, tomatoes, lettuce and onion and dripping with mayonnaise and hot sauce, he'd begun to suspect from her spotty records that Nicole Smith might have gone to great lengths to hide her past.

If anything, that intrigued him more than ever. He finished the sandwich, put her current address in his GPS and started toward her residence. Two blocks from the restaurant, he realized he was being followed.

Good old Lee. He didn't miss a trick. Remy ditched the tail long before he pulled up at the entrance to an exclusive, gated town-house complex. He followed a car inside and parked in Nicole's driveway. When she didn't answer her doorbell, he went back to his truck and tried to honestly examine his own motive for being there.

Was this only an excuse to see her again? Or did he really think it was necessary to warn her about Lee? Was it that he just couldn't bear to think of Lee Barnaby in a relationship with a woman who reminded Remy so much of Carlotta?

Memories of Carlotta pushed from the crevices of his subconsciousness and took over his mind. Without warning, Nicole's image merged with that of Carlotta's.

What the hell was wrong with him? Coming here had been a stupid, libido-driven mistake. Nicole was not Carlotta. Who she dated was none of his business, and there was no reason to think she was in any danger from Lee.

Remy shoved the key into the ignition and brought the motor to life. A red sports car pulled up behind him before he could switch the gear from Park to Reverse.

Nicole stepped out of her car. The sight of her stole every ounce of his resolve. Any thought of leaving flew from his mind.

NICOLE GULPED IN a steadying breath of air that did little to settle the unnerving excitement of seeing Andre standing in her driveway.

"This is a surprise," she said, trying for nonchalance but unable to block the pleasure from creeping into her voice.

"I hope you don't mind my just showing up," he said. "Say the word and I'll cut out."

"No, I'm glad you stopped by, though I can't imagine how you found me."

"All it took was a little research. Did I fail to mention that I'm a private detective?"

"Yes. But our conversation was brief. You never even got around to telling me your last name."

"Then let's start over and do this right. I'm Remy Comeaux. Pleased to meet you, Nicole Smith."

"I thought you said your name was Andre."

"That was when I was trying to keep anyone from telling Lee that I was there and spoiling my plan to just walk up and surprise him."

"And did you?"

"Absolutely. That's part of the reason I'm here."

And now that Lee's name had come up, this encounter felt a bit clandestine. She wondered if he were aware that she and Lee were dating.

He walked beside her on the narrow paved path to her door. His nearness was all but intoxicating, and when his arm brushed hers, desire vibrated along her never endings.

She moved away from him, determined to resist the bizarre attraction.

"I'm not much of a drinker," she said as they stepped into the high-ceilinged living area. "I may have a bit of whiskey and I have some chilled chardonnay and a bottle of nice pinot noir Lee brought over last week."

Mentioning Lee made her feel a little less as if she was orchestrating a seduction scene.

"Maybe we should talk first," he said.

"In that case, take a seat."

He took the sofa. She deliberately chose the chair farthest away from him. She crossed her legs. "If you're an insurance salesman, I'm covered to my eyeballs."

He grinned. "I'm not selling anything—or maybe I am, but it won't cost you any money."

Oh, no. Surely Lee hadn't sent him here to plead his case. If so, the new police chief should have chosen a far less enticing man to deliver his pitch.

"Did Lee send you?"

"No, actually, I misrepresented myself last night when we met. I'm not actually a friend of Lee's. I worked for him years ago. Before Katrina."

She had no idea where this was going. "Were you a police officer?"

"I was a narcotics detective."

"So exactly why are you here, Remy Comeaux—if that's your real name?"

"It's my real name." He rested his elbows on his knees and leaned in closer. "I don't know exactly what your relationship is with Lee Barnaby, Nicole, but just in case it's serious or about to become serious, I think you should know the truth about the man."

She grew uneasy, and this time it had nothing to do with attraction. "Lee's a friend of mine. If you're here to spread gossip or disparage him, I'd rather not hear it."

"I don't gossip and I don't knock any man without good cause. I hate having to tell you this, Nicole. I sincerely do, but now that I've met you, I can't just stand by and let you get hurt by a man like Lee Barnaby."

"What kind of man would that be? A dedicated public servant? A city leader?"

"Lee Barnaby is not the knight in police armor he portrays. He's corrupt to the core and has been for years."

"Corrupt in what way?"

"At the very least he takes bribes. And I have reason to believe his crimes could be a lot worse."

Her stomach knotted. She shouldn't listen to another word of these baseless accusations, not from a man she had no reason to trust. Even if Remy was sincere, that didn't mean he was right. He hadn't worked for the NOPD in years.

She uncrossed her legs and stood. "I think you should go now, Remy."

He stood but didn't walk away. When his gaze captured hers, her knees grew weak. Heaven help her, but even now, she felt the crazy urge to throw herself into his arms.

"I'm only telling you this for your own protection. You can do what you want with the information."

"Why would you think you should protect me? You don't know me. You don't owe me anything."

He crossed the room and stopped so near her that a hint of his musky, woodsy aftershave filled her senses. He took both of her hands in his. "I came because it was the right thing to do."

His lips were so close she was sure he was going to kiss her. Her insides melted into a pool of slick heat. This was absurd. She should back away.

But it was Remy who came to his senses. He let go of her hands and took a step backward. He removed a business card from his pocket and pressed it into her hand.

"If you need to talk," he said, his voice hoarse from what sounded a lot like desire, "if you need me for anything at all, just call."

He left her standing alone and staring after him as he let himself out her door. The click of his heels echoed around her. And suddenly the room felt incredibly empty without him in it.

She took a deep breath and struggled for a grip on reality as she read his card.

Remy Comeaux. Private Detective. The business address was in Houston, Texas.

Standing next to Remy and staring into his hypnotic eyes, it was easy to believe everything he said. But he'd lied about being Lee's friend. He'd even lied about his name. Why should she trust what he said now?

On impulse, she took her phone from her purse and punched in Lee's phone number. He was a friend. She owed him a chance to explain and defend himself against Remy's accusations.

Chapter Six

Nicole switched the bag holding cartons of Chinese food into her left hand and used her right to fit the key into Lee's front-door lock. Once inside, she quickly turned off the alarm system and made her way to the kitchen to unpack the food.

Lee had given her a key to his house over a month ago, the first time she was to meet him there for an early dinner. He'd explained that his schedule was so unpredictable that he never knew when he'd be detained.

He'd also encouraged her to come over and make use of his pool anytime. He'd even shown her where he kept a hidden key to the back door just in case she locked herself out, and a key to the privacy-fence gate in case she wanted to stroll along the shady path that meandered through his country-club neighborhood.

He had a reputation for being tough on criminals and running the department with an iron hand, but he had never been anything but thoughtful with her. His patience was starting to wear thin with her unwillingness to be intimate with him. But he'd been a lot slower at reaching that point than other men she'd dated.

Only, where was that reluctance with Remy? Would she have pulled away if he'd kissed her tonight, or would she have thrown herself at him like a sex-starved nympho?

Thankfully, she hadn't been put to the test.

Nicole set the table while she waited for Lee. Then she lit candles and put out wineglasses, creating a setting that she hoped would open the lines of communication regarding Remy.

She left the choice of wines from his extensive selection to Lee. The man did live well. While his spacious home in the Metairie Country Club neighborhood was nowhere near as extravagantly furnished as the Delacroixes', it had the handprint of one of the city's most prominent decorators embedded in every detail.

But then, he didn't have to live on his salary. His father had been a very successful shipping magnate before he and Lee's mother had died in a private plane crash while flying to their Cape Cod estate.

Nicole walked out the back door, took a bottle of water from the refrigerator in his outdoor kitchen and then kicked out of her shoes. She took a beach towel and spread it on the side of his magnificent pool so that she could sit and dangle her feet in the cool water. Kids' laughter and voices drifted from the other side of the six-foot privacy fence.

Lee's world.

Lee Barnaby, the ultimate cop, the celebrated new chief of police, a slave to the law, always driven to keep his city safe. She'd never had any reason to believe he was anything less.

Until Remy had stepped into her life.

She had no reason to believe the ex-cop turned private eye. Yet his need to protect her seemed so convincing. Why else would he have come to see her? Certainly not to seduce her, or he would have at least kissed her when she was practically drooling.

After ten minutes of agonizing, she went back inside. A phone was ringing, but it wasn't the one in the kitchen. Still, she should find and answer it in case it was Lee saying how much longer he'd be delayed or if he had to cancel their evening together.

She located the piercing instrument at the end of the hallway in what appeared to be Lee's home office. Before she could answer it, the caller hung up.

The light on the answering machine was blinking. Maybe it had been Lee and he'd left a message. She pressed the button.

There were two calls, neither from Lee. One was from someone named Mia, and the call sounded urgent. Nicole recognized the prefix as being from the Cayman Islands only because Dr. Cantrell and his wife, Leslie, had just returned from vacationing there. As his office manager, she'd had to call him several times on business matters.

Perhaps Lee was planning a trip there, as well. Or else he had business there—or investments. There were countless legitimate reasons for him to have received that call.

Still, suspicions began to bounce around in her mind. If Lee were guilty of taking bribes, he might use a bank in the Islands to hide the extra income.

Impulsively, she pulled her cell phone from her pocket and called the number that had been left on Lee's machine. She reached a recorded message that explained the bank was closed for normal business hours and provided another number in case of an emergency. A sinking feeling settled in the pit of her stomach.

"Hello, my sweet."

Nicole jumped at the sound of Lee's voice.

"I didn't mean to startle you," he said.

"I didn't hear you come in."

"Apparently. So what are you doing back here in my office?"

"The phone was ringing. I thought it might be you trying to reach me."

His brows arched. "Had I wanted you, I'd have called your cell phone."

"I was poolside for a few minutes. I thought I might have missed a call from you saying why you were running late."

"I'm sorry. I guess I should have gotten in touch. There's been one emergency after another today. Since you checked, did I have any messages that sounded important?"

"I couldn't say. I punched the skip button as soon as I realized the messages weren't from you."

He smiled, and for the first time since he'd arrived, he appeared to relax. He put an arm around her waist and kissed her on the mouth. As usual, she felt nothing. The total opposite of Remy's almost kiss.

"The messages can wait," he said. "I'm starved and I smell Chinese food. I'm glad you decided to come over tonight. Like I said, it's been a hell of a day."

As they ate, Lee detailed a run-in with the D.A. and a problem one of his best detectives was having with a brutality accusation. Nicole only half listened as she forced down a few bites of food.

She waited until Lee's plate was almost empty before tackling the subject that had stolen her appetite.

"Did Remy Comeaux ever find you at the party last evening?"

Lee's demeanor changed in an instant. His muscles strained and veins popped out on his forehead as if just the name enraged him. "How do you know Remy Comeaux?"

"I don't really know him." Not actually a lie. "I met him at the Delacroixes'. He said he was a close friend of yours."

Lee muttered a string of curses. "Why didn't you tell me last night that you'd met him?"

"It slipped my mind. There was a lot going on."

"Believe me, Remy is no friend. He had no business being there and even less business harassing you."

"He didn't harass me. We only exchanged a few words." No reason to mention that she'd initiated it.

"I don't suppose he told you that he's a dirty cop I had arrested eight years ago, just before Katrina hit."

"Did he do jail time?"

"No. Unfortunately the evidence against him was lost in the resulting floods, the same as it was in a lot of other cases. Remy left town and I had far more important matters to tend to at that point than a cop who'd disgraced his badge."

"Why do you think he's come back to town now?" she questioned.

"To cause trouble for me."

"Why? You'd think he'd just be glad he escaped prosecution."

"It's a vendetta with him. His girlfriend drowned in the flooding or else she just took advantage of the opportunity to dump him. Anyway, he blames me for that."

"Because you'd had him arrested?"

"Right. He claimed he'd have been there to keep her safe if he hadn't been behind bars. More likely he'd have been looting a local business while the owners fled to safety. Remy Comeaux is bad news and always has been. If he comes anywhere near you, call me. I'll take care of it from there."

"Are you *ordering* me not to talk to him?"

"For you own good."

She'd never seen this side of Lee. If having Remy in town upset him this much, it made Remy's accusations seem a lot more credible.

Lee pushed his plate away and stood. "Food was great, but I've had enough. Talk of Remy would make any man lose his appetite. And unfortunately, I've got to go back down to headquarters to look at some reports."

"You should have told me you have to work tonight. We could have had dinner together another time."

"I wanted to see you, and a man has to eat."

Only, he didn't look that glad to see her now. He looked distracted and distant, and fury continued to strain every line in his face.

Whatever had happened between Lee and Remy went far deeper than just a botched arrest from years ago.

"Why don't you go check your messages while I clean off the table?" she offered.

"Okay, but just rinse the dishes and leave them in the sink. The cleaning woman can take care of the rest in the morning. She's only here half a day on Tuesdays, but that's long enough to clean the kitchen."

"It only takes a few minutes more to put them in the dishwasher."

"Suit yourself."

By the time Lee returned to the kitchen, everything was as spotless as she'd found it.

"I ought to have that phone disconnected," Lee said. "All I get on it are nuisance calls."

"I take it the messages weren't important."

"People wanting contributions."

Nicole doubted that a bank in the Cayman Islands was looking for a donation.

When Lee walked her to her car, she was more confused than ever. Remy's words haunted her all the way home. Not only did he insist that Lee was corrupt and guilty of taking bribes, but that he could be guilty of something even worse.

But how much worse?

The only way to find out was to talk to Remy again.

REMY WAS UP AND ON the job early Tuesday morning. He finally caught up with Reggio Sanchez in Algiers. He was out back of the house in a cloud of marijuana smoke while he watched two men strip the tires from a Buick that was up on blocks. Remy figured the car was stolen.

Reggio greeted Remy's arrival with a flick of the joint that dangled from his lips. "What took you so long, Comeaux? I could tell by the smell you were back in town."

"Yeah. Couldn't stay away from the old gang."

Reggio sneered. "I hear you been running all over town trying to find me. You got business with me?"

"Just hoping to catch a preview of your latest action flick. Heard it was based on your visit to Jessie Klein the morning you filled her with lead."

"As usual, you got your facts wrong." Reggio took a long drag and blew the smoke Remy's way. "Movie was all police fabrication. I was out of town the day poor, lying Jessie Klein got shot."

"That's not what Doyle Shriver said."

"Should have known he'd be a friend of yours. You dirty cops have a union or something?"

"Did you kill Shriver, too?"

"No. Had no reason to. I hear he left one swell-looking widow, though. May have to drop by and give her a little comfort. Show her what a real man's like."

"You lay one finger on Syl Shriver, Sanchez, and I'll personally see that you get run up the flagpole in front of city hall."

The two men who'd pretended not to be listening stepped away from the car as if on cue. One had a pistol stuck in the waistband of his ragged-edged cutoffs.

Remy had no doubt the other was also toting. Probably had knives on them, as well, as would Reggio.

Remy had no intention of taking them on. He didn't care for the odds. But if he had to defend himself, his own pistol was in easy reach, resting in the shoulder holster under his lightweight windbreaker.

Reggio leaned against the front fender of the Buick, grinning as if he found this whole encounter a big joke.

"Sounds like you got the hots for the woman yourself. Guess you finally got over that bitch you were screwing before Katrina. I heard some of my bros had a real good time with her before they dumped her in the bayou."

Remy lost control in an instant. The first punch sent Reggio doubling over with pain.

The click of cocking triggers brought him back into focus. In a heartbeat the short barrel of his automatic was pressed against Reggio's right temple.

"Put 'em away, bros," Reggio ordered. "This is between me and Comeaux. We're just expressin' a difference of opinion."

"Toss your guns into that wooded area behind the house," Remy ordered. "Reggio here will walk me to my truck. Always nice to have the kind of friend who'll watch my back."

The men hesitated until Reggio nodded his okay. Even then it was clear they were not too happy about complying.

Remy lowered his gun but kept it in hand with his finger on the trigger as he and Reggio rounded the corner of the wood-frame house and walked to his truck.

"Tell your buddy the new chief of police hello for me," Remy said as he climbed behind the wheel. "And then you'd be wise to hire the best lawyer all that drug money can buy. Your high-powered partner in crime is going down, and he might just take you along for the crash."

"Talk's cheap, Comeaux. You aren't tough enough to play in this city. You never were."

Remy let the comment ride. Talk was cheap. It was time for action.

The son of a bitch's arrogance told Remy all he needed to know. Reggio was definitely guilty. He'd killed Jessie and likely Doyle, as well. Remy had a hunch the latter was at Lee's bidding.

If he could prove that, no jury in Louisiana would let the il-lustrious police chief or Reggio Sanchez walk free.

His phone rang just as he pulled into a drive-through burger joint for a cup of brew to go. He yanked the phone from his pocket, hoping the call would be from Ray Storm or Mack Rivet. His former partners in the original investigation of Lee Barnaby were both proving to be more difficult to track down than he'd expected.

The caller ID said Nicole Smith.

Surprise and pleasure battled for front and center.

Even though he'd told her to call if she needed anything at all, he hadn't expected to hear from her. "Hello."

"Remy, it's Nicole. I hate to bother you, but I think this could be important."

The alarm in her voice put the pleasure on hold. "It's not a bother. What's up?"

"Can you meet me at my office? It's downtown and easy to get to."

"Sure."

He would have found a way to meet her if she'd said she was on the moon.

Chapter Seven

Remy spotted Nicole on the corner near the intersection where she'd told him to meet her. She looked good enough to stop traffic in a straight black skirt that showed off her hips and legs to perfection.

Her white blouse was topped with a pale yellow cardigan that fell just below her waist. Her red hair shone in the midday sun like silken fire.

He checked his rearview mirror to make certain there was no sign of the car that had been tailing him when he left his hotel that morning. He couldn't chance pulling Nicole into any danger.

She waved as he stopped and leaned over to open the passenger door. Her skirt inched up her thighs as she got in. His libido took notice. He looked away before his arousal got out of hand.

He pulled back into a line of slow-moving traffic. "I didn't expect to hear from you again after last night."

"I didn't expect to call," she admitted.

"I hope it's not trouble that changed your mind."

"At this point, it's just concern. Have you had lunch?"

"No, or breakfast, either. But why is it I think you didn't call to make sure I'm eating right?"

"Must be that detective intuition. But there's a good Italian restaurant nearby that's usually not too busy on Tuesdays. It should be quiet enough to talk there."

"Just point the way."

She didn't volunteer more and he didn't ask until they'd been seated and served tall glasses of sweet iced tea. He sensed her uneasiness and picked up a few very bad vibes.

"Is this meeting Lee's idea?"

Her face registered surprise. "No. Why would you think Lee would want me to see you?"

"Just a hunch. I'm glad I'm wrong."

Her manicured nails tapped the printed luncheon menu. "I did have dinner with Lee last night, but I only mentioned our few-second conversation at the party."

"So why did you call me today?"

"I have questions that I need answered."

"Shoot."

"Lee says you were a dirty cop. Were you?"

"No. I was so clean, in fact, that the FBI had asked me to help them with an ongoing investigation involving corruption inside the NOPD."

"You didn't mention the FBI last night."

"You didn't give me much of a chance." He explained his involvement in the investigation as succinctly as he could. She listened without interruption, but he still wasn't sure she believed him.

The waitress returned, interrupting the discussion. Nicole ordered a salad. Remy glanced at the specials board and took the first thing on the list. He figured he couldn't go wrong with spaghetti and meatballs.

Nicole worried the handle of her fork for a few seconds before looking up. "What were you referring to last night when you said that Lee might be guilty of something even worse than taking bribes?"

He hesitated, hating the prospect of diving into the depraved details of Doyle Shriver's death with her. "All I have is speculation, Nicole. Nothing I can say will be any more convincing than what I told you last night."

She ran a finger up and down her icy glass, smearing the condensation and pushing it into tiny rivers of moisture. "It might. I discovered something last night that made your accusations a bit more credible."

Nicole recounted her call to the bank in the Cayman Islands and the fact that Lee had lied about the messages on his phone.

"You called a bank in the Cayman Islands from Lee's phone?"

"No. I made the call from my phone, but I didn't leave a message."

Remy had only meant to protect her. Instead he might have pulled her into danger.

"I should never have said a word to you about this," he said. "You have to stay out of this. Don't give Lee any reason not to trust you."

"Then level with me. Other than taking bribes, what other crimes do you think Lee's committed? If you don't tell me the truth, I'll find out on my own."

And that could get her killed, the same as it had gotten Jessie Klein and Doyle Shriver killed.

He studied Nicole across the table. Her features were delicate, yet there was a whispered strength in them as well, as if her alabaster complexion was only a mask that covered a will of steel. Perhaps it was that as much as the red hair and tantalizing, lyrical laugh that reminded him so much of Carlotta.

He took a deep breath and plunged ahead. "I think that Lee may have had one of his own officers assassinated."

Her eyes widened in horror but her gaze didn't waver. "Doyle Shriver?"

Remy's concern accelerated. "What do you know about that?"

"I know his wife, Syl. She was a nurse in Dr. Cantrell's office before she got pregnant with Toby. And he's the only cop who's been murdered by an unknown assailant recently."

"What did Syl tell you about his death?"

"Nothing that made a lot of sense, but she mentioned something about missing film and not trusting Lee. I figured it was just her grief talking. You surely don't think Lee had something to do with Doyle's death?"

"I can't say any more, Nicole, but I'm begging you to stay out of this."

"I'm afraid I can't do that. But I'll make a deal with you."

"No deals. The situation is too dangerous."

"Lee has a home office with lots of file cabinets," she continued as if she hadn't heard him. "The missing film or at least some evidence of its veracity might be in those files."

"Or it might not be. Either way, you're not breaking and entering to look for it."

"I won't have to. I have keys to Lee's house and the code for his alarm system. We can go through the front door or sneak in the back if we can find a way for one of us to scale a high privacy fence."

"Did you even hear what I said about this situation being too dangerous?"

"I heard you. Here's my deal. Either you go with me or I go alone, take a peek at his files and see if I can figure out for myself if the guy is the monster you portray him as. Are you in or out?"

"You do believe in cutting to the chase."

"It's a gift."

The waitress returned with their food before he could argue the point. But somehow he knew that further verbal confrontation would be useless. Nicole was apparently not only gorgeous but also spunky as hell.

She'd called his bluff. No way would he let her go snooping in Lee Barnaby's house alone, not when he was the one who'd dragged her into his war.

Chapter Eight

"That's Lee's house just ahead." Nicole pointed to the two-story white Colonial with the dark green shutters.

"Impressive bachelor pad." Remy slowed the truck. "No cars in the driveway."

"Which means the cleaning woman has come and gone," Nicole said. "It should be clear sailing for a few hours."

"Unless Lee decides to return home for some reason in the middle of the afternoon," Remy countered.

"Are you always such a pessimist?"

"In my line of work we call it survival. And it's not like the police chief punches a clock."

Nonetheless, Remy continued to the corner, turned left and then turned again onto a street one block west of Lee's house, just as she'd suggested on the drive over. He pulled to the curb and parked beneath a canopy of branches heralding spring with their burst of new leaves.

Nicole shifted and opened the door of the truck, stepping carefully to avoid tripping on the gnarled roots that crawled away in every direction from a huge tree trunk. A squirrel scurried out of her way before racing up the ragged trunk. Birds sang from perches far above her. The sky was cloudless.

Her nerves were the only hint that she was on shaky ground and she was determined not to let Remy see her uneasiness. Two days ago she would have never considered breaking into anyone's house, much less one owned by the chief of police. Her life had been as predictable as the ending of last year's reruns. It had been ordinary, safe—and boring.

Enter Remy Comeaux and suddenly she was not only flirting with *him* but danger, as well. She wondered what Deanie would think if she could see her now. Most likely she'd be cheering her on. But she couldn't tell even Deanie about this.

If all went as planned, no one would ever know she was involved in any of this. That was Remy's stipulation to the deal.

Nicole led the way to the corner entry to the hiking trail that ran behind Lee's house. Minutes later, the second floor and the privacy fence that surrounded his backyard and pool came into view. The fence looked to be an insurmountable obstacle to her. Thankfully, there was always the front-door option.

"Still think you can scale that?"

He looked up, eyeing the overhanging branches. "Sure. I scampered up trees like that down in the bayou half my life."

She wrapped her arms around her chest. "You'll have quite a drop on the other side."

"Not too bad." He pointed to the branches that hung over the fence. "I can drop to a lower branch once I'm on the chief's turf."

"Just don't expect me to follow. You'll have to retrieve the gate key and come back for me."

"Don't tell me you're afraid of heights."

"Not as long as I have both feet on terra firma."

His teasing smile faded from his face. "It's not too late to back out of all of this."

Nicole considered it for about half a second. If Lee was half as evil as Remy suspected, there was nothing to keep him from shooting Remy on the spot if he came home and found him there. If Lee declared he was defending himself against an intruder, no one would question him.

But she couldn't believe he would shoot her. They were friends. He cared for her. Besides, killing your girlfriend would require a lot more explaining. And he wouldn't risk shooting Remy if she was there as a witness.

Arrest him, sure. But not shoot him. Unless Remy gave him reason… "Tell me you're not carrying a weapon under that windbreaker, Remy."

"Just a small semiautomatic .45."

Horror swept through her. She hadn't considered possible gunfire when she'd concocted this plan.

"I'm teasing, Nicole. I left my weapon in the truck. I'm not stupid enough to give Lee an armed-burglary charge to use against me. I'm not taking you to a gunfight."

"Good."

"You shouldn't be here anyway. You don't have a dog in the fight."

"You're not the only person interested in justice, Remy Comeaux." And the truth was she didn't want to play it smart or safe. She'd done that for years, always thinking her life was on the verge of taking off but never quite getting there.

Now she was actually taking a risk, doing something that wasn't expected of her, fighting for a cause bigger than herself. Her nerves might be shot, but she'd never felt more alive.

"You said you had to protect me because it was the right thing to do, Remy. Well, I have to do this for the same reason."

Remy met her defiant gaze straight on and then reached for her hand and squeezed it. "Point made, but I'd still rather you go back and wait in the truck."

"Not going to happen." She pulled on the pair of latex gloves that Remy had given her.

Then, true to his word, Remy shinnied up the tree with the skill and agility of an eight-year-old. She barely breathed until she heard him drop to the soft, grassy earth of Lee's back lawn.

She clasped Lee's door key in her right hand until she heard the click of the gate as it opened.

"Last chance to back out," Remy said.

"Thanks, but no thanks."

They crossed the small yard quickly. Once inside the house, she punched in the code for the back-door alarm pad and took a deep breath as the warning beep gave way to silence.

They were inside. The house was empty. If they moved quickly, they could clear out before anyone knew they'd been there.

Now, if they could just find something to back up Remy's accusations—if Lee was actually guilty. She still wanted to believe that he was the man of honor she and most of New Orleans had always thought him to be, but Remy's arguments were persuasive.

If Lee had ordered Doyle killed, he'd likely already planned the same fate for Remy. Her blood ran cold at the thought.

"Leave the back door open," she said, "in case we have to make a fast escape." She started toward Lee's office, but Remy didn't follow.

He lingered and scanned the area. "A man would have to be drawing a hell of a salary to live like this."

"He probably bought and furnished the house with family money," she said, trying to at least be fair.

"Not unless he bought himself a new family."

"I don't know what you mean. His father was a shipping magnate. He must have inherited a small fortune."

"His dad was an appliance repairman from Jersey and his mother died when he was ten."

"Are you sure?"

"Dead certain. The FBI had that info before Katrina. Now, let's get started."

"You'll have to give me some guidelines about what I'm searching for," Nicole said as they reached the office. "I'm thinking mortgages or bank-deposit slips or maybe some notation about Lee's communication with drug dealers."

"That would help," Remy agreed. "But what I'd really like to recover is the missing film that shows Reggio Sanchez at the scene of Jessie Klein's murder."

"I just hope he kept it and that it's here."

"He'd have to keep it somewhere—as a bargaining tool to use against Reggio. Besides, men as arrogant as Lee who've scammed the world as long as he has believe they're above getting caught."

"Can you use evidence obtained illegally in a trial?"

"If we were cops, we'd need a search warrant. But I can guarantee you that Lee is never going to admit the film was stolen from him."

"If we do find it, who will you give it to?"

"My first choice would be Ray Storm. He's the FBI agent I was working with before Katrina. But I've been trying to reach him for days without success. I suspect he's on an undercover assignment."

"And your second choice?"

"The highest-ranking agent in the local FBI office."

"You have it all worked out, don't you?"

"I've had years to think about taking Lee down. I just never expected it to involve murder."

Lee had been right about one thing. This was a vendetta for Remy. He must have loved the woman who was killed in Katrina very much.

"Has Lee ever mentioned or shown you a hidden safe?" Remy asked.

"No."

"Then we'll start in Lee's office."

Their first discovery was that the large desk drawer and a freestanding wooden file cabinet were both locked.

"No big deal," Remy assured her. He pulled a toothpick-size tool from his pocket. "I just want to do as little damage as possible so that Lee won't realize right away that we tampered with the locks. We don't want to tip him off so that he gets rid of evidence we might not find before the FBI has a chance to seize everything."

"That makes sense."

"You start with the desk," Remy said as soon as he released the lock. "I'll take the file cabinet. If you see anything at all suspicious, show it to me."

Nicole worked quickly, absorbed in the task but jumping at every unfamiliar sound. The click of the motor when the air conditioner turned itself on or off. The drop of cubes from the ice maker. The chime of the grandfather clock in the entryway.

The ring of the doorbell.

Her heart pounded in her chest as she jumped away from the desk.

"Stay calm," Remy whispered. "Lee wouldn't be ringing his own doorbell. Whoever it is will assume no one's home and go away."

"Unless they have a key, as I do."

The bell rang again.

Remy went to the window and peeked around the blind. "There's a UPS truck parked in the street in front of the house. It's just a delivery."

She exhaled slowly, still holding on to the edge of Lee's desk with clammy hands. "Have you found anything helpful?" she asked, hoping this foray into the dark side wasn't futile.

"A deed for a very pricey estate in Montego Bay, perhaps a retirement property in case things get too hot for him here. Turn on his laptop and see if you can bring up his email."

She tried but got nowhere. "I need a password to get into the computer."

"That figures. Play around with it while I search for a hidden safe. The files are too clean. Lee has to have somewhere else he keeps his dirty records."

"How do you even start looking for a hidden safe?"

"Look for telltale evidence. Slightly crooked pictures. Furniture at odd angles as if it were hurriedly shoved back into place. Other than that, it's just a crapshoot."

"You'd have made a great burglar."

"Always nice to have options in case the P.I. gig doesn't pan out."

"In the meantime, we need to hurry it up," Nicole reminded him. "Lee could get home anytime, especially if he has to attend an event tonight."

"I'll risk it. You shouldn't." He reached in the front jeans pocket and pulled out a rattling key ring. "Here's my truck keys. Clear out now and drive to a nearby coffee shop. I'll call when I'm done."

And risk Remy being shot as an intruder? No way. "I've started this. I'll finish it."

She spent the next half hour at the computer with zero luck. Everything was password protected, and her attempts at guessing his were futile. Finally she gave up and went to help Remy search for a safe.

She followed him from room to room, watched his muscles flex as he moved huge pieces of art and scooted furniture around as if they were kids' blocks. His strength was as amazing as his determination.

Finally she went off on her own, stopping at the door to Lee's bedroom. She stared at the king-size bed. If she had given in to Lee's pleas, they would have been lovers in that bed. Between those very sheets. Her stomach churned.

She was about to back away when she noticed something odd about the fireplace. She walked over for a closer look. Not only was it a fake structure, but it held gas logs that looked as if they'd never been burned.

The whole setup lacked the elegance of the rest of the room. She doubted his designer had had a say in installing it.

"Come in here a minute," she called. "I think I may have found something."

Hesitant to hope for too much, she tried to ignore her sky-rocketing pulse as Remy scrutinized the fireplace and even the logs. Finally he located a control knob attached to one of the fake logs.

One turn and the fireplace swiveled, revealing a metal safe big enough for a baby to crawl into.

Nicole gave a whoop and then quickly slapped her hand over her mouth in horror that she'd been so noisy. "We did it," she whispered.

"Not quite," Remy said. "We still have to get this baby open."

"You have tools."

"But this isn't a cheap safe. My tools may be no match for this lock."

She chewed her fingernails and prayed as he worked. The combination lock didn't budge.

The clock in the hall chimed five times.

"Okay, Nicole. If you won't leave, I need you to stand guard at the front window and watch for Lee to return. If you see him drive up, call to me and then run like hell. Go out the back door and out the back gate and I'll meet you at the truck."

"And if you don't?"

"I will. I promise, I'll be right behind you. Please don't argue with me this time, Nicole. There's no time to waste."

And then he kissed her quick but hard on the mouth. She dissolved in heat and need and hunger for him, stronger than she could remember ever having felt before.

This had to work. They had to get out of here safely. If Remy ended up in jail or worse because of her idea to come here, she'd never forgive herself.

The minutes dragged by as she waited for Remy and watched for Lee.

She recognized Lee's car even before it turned in the driveway. Terror gripped her, and instead of running to the back door, she ran to the bedroom.

"Lee's home. Let's go."

Remy was squatted on his haunches, rummaging through an *open* safe.

"We may have hit pay dirt." He held up a DVD and then quickly slipped it into an inside pocket of his windbreaker.

"Great, now let's go."

"Right behind you," he said, scooping up more contents. "Just have to close the safe and move everything back in place."

"There's no time."

"Okay." He stood and gave her a gentle shove toward the door. "Move it. I'm right behind you."

The clattering grind of the garage door's motor started just as she made it to the back door. She didn't slow down until she reached the gate in the privacy fence.

She looked back. Remy was nowhere in sight.

Chapter Nine

Nicole closed the gate and leaned against it. Anxiety clawed at her control. Remy had said he'd be right behind her. So where was he?

Had he gone back for something? Was he facing Lee and a police-issued pistol right now? Had Remy lied about being unarmed and stayed behind to lure Lee into a showdown?

If someone gets shot, please don't let it be Remy.

Her worries were all for him. How could that possibly be when he was more phantom than reality in her life? He haunted her thoughts and dreams, but the man himself was a mysterious stranger.

But there was no denying the fear that clutched at her heart like spiky pincers. She finally stepped away from the gate and began the long walk back to the truck.

She made one staggering step before two strong arms wound around her from the back. Panic made her gasp for breath.

"What's wrong, Nicole? Are you hurt?"

"Remy? You scared me to death. Where were you? Why didn't you come?"

"I went to the truck like we said."

She pulled away from his grasp. "You *said* you'd be right behind me."

"I would have been, but by the time the safe was closed and the fireplace in order, Lee was already in the house."

"Did he see you?"

"No. Fortunately, he went straight to the kitchen and then I heard the back door open. I figured he'd grabbed a beer and stepped out onto the deck. I hoped to God you hadn't waited around, but I figured if you had, he'd have been thrilled that you'd stopped by."

"He didn't see me. I ran, like you were supposed to do."

"I ran—just in the opposite direction. Once I'd covered my tracks, I opened the bedroom window and jumped out. But don't worry. I closed it behind me and even tapped the screen back in place. We're home free—at least for now."

The fear dimmed enough that her thoughts began to clear. "Do you really have the missing evidence film?"

"I found a DVD that could be it. I'll have to get back to my truck and my laptop to know for sure. But that's not all I found."

"What else?"

"Let's start back to the truck and I'll tell you all about it." He tugged her around so that they were heading in the opposite direction.

She'd been so upset she hadn't known her right from her left. It didn't surprise her. Remy had her world spinning on a new axis, out of control. Taking risks. Deliriously infatuated.

Except for the danger, she hoped it would never end.

INSTEAD OF TRYING TO WATCH the video in the cramped truck, Remy had agreed with Nicole's suggestion to go back and watch it in Dr. Cantrell's office. It was after hours. They'd have the place to themselves.

Remy was impressed with the classy setup. Cantrell was obviously a very successful plastic surgeon.

He made a quick pit stop while Nicole started a pot of coffee. By the time she rejoined him in her office, two cups of steaming brew in hand, he had the DVD in the computer and ready to roll.

She pulled a chair up next to his. "I'm almost afraid to look."

"It shouldn't be too gory. The missing film was from the outside camera, so it won't show the body or the murder itself."

"I mean I'm afraid to look because it might be pictures of Lee winning some award instead of Reggio Sanchez."

Remy clicked Play. "We'll soon find out."

The first shots were of an empty alleyway. A cat cast shadows in the dawn's first light as it jumped from one trash can to another. Headlights that looked to be from a passing car briefly lit the scene.

A second later, a woman wearing a black coat and carrying

an oversize handbag entered from the right. Her shoulders were slightly stooped, her short hair gray and frizzed.

"Bingo. That's Jessie Klein," Remy said.

"How do you know?"

"I did my research."

Just as she unlocked the back door of the diner, a tall man wearing baggy jeans and a light-colored T-shirt strode into the picture. Tattoos spiraled from his wrists, ducking beneath his short sleeves before curling up his neck. He needed a shave.

Remy paused the video for a better look. "That's Reggio Sanchez, a son of a bitch who's been terrorizing anyone who crosses him for decades."

"How did Jessie cross him?"

"She didn't. Her grandson did and she witnessed his murder and named Reggio as the triggerman. She was a reliable eyewitness who apparently didn't let Reggio frighten her into keeping quiet."

"So he made sure she wouldn't testify," Nicole said. "And Lee Barnaby got rid of the proof needed to send Reggio to jail for the rest of his life."

"Revolting, but true."

Nicole stared into space. "You read about things like this, but you never expect it from a person you know, especially when that person is a charismatic leader who reeks of success."

"Greed and power are no respecters of persons." Remy pushed Play again.

Reggio rushed from behind, put a meaty hand over Jessie's mouth and shoved her into the restaurant, kicking the door shut behind him. Less than five minutes later, he exited the same door. He had a pistol in his left hand and was shoving a muffin into his mouth with the other. Dark stains, so wet they were still dripping, covered the front of his shirt.

Nicole covered her eyes as if the images were too much to bear.

"So much for his airtight alibi," Remy said.

"Hopefully this will finally send the murderous thug to prison,"

Nicole said. "But I still have difficulty believing that Lee could be a part of any of that."

"He'll get a trial. If a jury agrees with you, he'll go free."

"But if he's guilty, I don't want him to go free." She got up and paced the room. "What else did you find in that safe?"

"Incriminating bank statements from two banks outside the country. And a list of dealers with how much Lee has received from each of them for the past ten years. Drugs are a very lucrative business for the former deputy chief of police, and there's no reason to think he has any intention of cleaning up his act now that he's been promoted to head honcho."

"So will you just go back to your hotel tonight?"

"Not to the same hotel. Lee's had someone tailing me since Sunday night. If he realizes the video is gone, he'll come after me, and I'm taking no chances with the film."

Nicole walked over and perched on the corner of the desk near his computer. "Take my car, Remy. I can get a taxi home and back to work in the morning. You can even stay at my place if you like. I have an extra bedroom."

Spend the night at Nicole's town house? It was a great offer, the best he'd had in years. But he couldn't take her up on it for so many reasons he couldn't begin to count them all. Mostly he didn't trust himself to deal with sensual desires he could barely control when he and Nicole were in public.

"I don't think my staying at your place is a good idea."

"Then I have another option. Dr. Cantrell and his wife live in Covington, but they keep a pied-à-terre in the French Quarter. I can make a quick phone call and see if it's available. I know he keeps a key to it in his office."

"Didn't you mention they were good friends with Lee? Under those circumstances, my staying there is not a good idea."

"I won't mention your name. I'll just say you're a friend of mine. It's the perfect solution, Remy. My car. The Cantrells' condo. You'll be flying far below the radar, especially since Lee has no reason to think I ignored his order not to see you again."

It did make sense, but... "Are you sure you want to stick your neck out even further, Nicole?"

"If Lee ever finds out I helped you, my neck will already be on the chopping block. What's another inch or two?"

"The difference between keeping or losing your head."

"A moot point. Lee will never know. Help yourself to more coffee, if you like. The pot is just down the hallway in the lounge. I'll make that call."

He watched her walk away and felt an immediate stirring in his groin. She was so damn much like Carlotta that it hurt to look at her.

The sensual sway of her hips. The way her hair danced about her shoulders. Shapely legs. Delectable lips. Gorgeous eyes. She was stunning in every way.

But there was a lot more to her than her looks. She'd proved that today. He could stick around when this was over and see how hot and high the flames could get.

He wouldn't. She deserved more than a man who couldn't look at her without visualizing another woman in his mind. Knowing he'd best keep his mind on the business at hand, he took out his phone and punched in the private phone number of the local head of the FBI. The sooner the video was in his hands, the more confident Remy would feel about Lee's impending arrest.

Nicole returned a few minutes later, a smile on her face and a small key ring dangling from her fingers. "It's all set. I don't think we should leave your truck in this parking garage, though. I don't want to cause any trouble for Dr. Cantrell."

"No, I'll park in a French Quarter lot and hang out for a while, make sure I'm not followed to the exclusive little pied-à-terre."

"And I'll drive straight to their condo and leave my car in their private parking space. I'll take a taxi home from there. I've been to the apartment many times. No one will think it odd to see my car there. But won't you have to go by your hotel to pick up your things?"

"Nope. I travel light, especially when I'm working a job. I've got a change of clothes, a toothbrush and a razor in the truck."

"Then how about a sandwich and another cup of coffee before you go? There's a deli next door that delivers. I've used them frequently when working late."

"I'm not sure that's a good idea." Not the way she was affecting him.

"You have to eat."

True, but it was another kind of hunger he was fighting now. Still, he didn't have the heart or the willpower to tell her no.

She ordered the sandwiches while he poured the coffee. As soon as they settled in comfortable chairs and she opened a new conversation, he knew he should have left.

"The woman you were in love with, the one who died in Katrina—what was she like, Remy?"

There was no real reason not to tell her the truth. He could talk about it now without breaking down. But how would he begin to describe Carlotta? He was pretty sure saying she was a lot like Nicole would be a major mistake.

He sat back and let his thoughts become words. "Carlotta walked into a room and it was like opening the skies and letting the sunshine free. She made even mundane things exciting. And when she laughed, it was downright hypnotic. There was no way not to laugh with her. She laughed a lot."

"How did you meet?"

"I took a bullet to my…" No way to say it delicately, so he patted his butt. "Carlotta was the nurse who took care of me in the hospital. From the moment I saw her, I was hooked. Amazingly, she fell for me just as fast."

"Not so amazing. You have a very seductive way about you."

"There are lots of people who wouldn't agree with you."

"Like Lee."

"Exactly."

"How did Carlotta die?"

"I don't know. That's one of the things that torments me most. The storm was over. She should have been heading to work about the time the levees were breached. Water reached the rooftops in the area surrounding the hospital where she worked. Knowing Carlotta, I'm sure she died trying to save someone."

"And you were in jail and couldn't save her."

"In jail on trumped-up charges that would never have held.

When the jail started to flood, someone unlocked my cell and I walked out."

"Did the police have her fingerprints?"

He nodded. "All the hospital employees had been finger-printed. I checked every day for months. No one matching her description or with her fingerprints was ever found."

"How terrible for you."

He'd said enough. He wasn't looking for pity. There was no point going into the pure hell he'd lived through, searching and refusing to believe Carlotta could be dead.

"Now you know my story," he said, cutting her off before she could ask more questions. "Tell me about you."

She shrugged. "There's not a lot to tell. I'm single, live alone and work for Dr. Cantrell."

Remy would have pressed for more had the arrival of the sandwiches not interrupted the conversation. They both became quiet after that. He finished his sandwich quickly and then they walked to their vehicles. He lingered as he opened her door for her. And then he looked into those mesmerizing green eyes and he started to melt.

His lips were touching hers before he could stop himself. She wrapped her arms around his neck and kissed him back. The need he'd been fighting took over and he got lost in the heat and passion.

His hands splayed her back and he pulled her closer and closer until she was pressed against his erection, his lips still ravishing hers. When she came up for air, his whole body was throbbing.

"Oh, Carlotta."

Nicole jerked away as if he'd slapped her.

His brain kicked back in.

"I'm sorry. I'm really sorry, Nicole."

"It's okay. I understand. Truly, I do."

But he'd hurt her and that was the last thing he'd wanted to do. Right now all he knew was that he had to leave before he did or said something else they might both regret.

He was falling hard. But was it for Nicole—or was he turning her into Carlotta in his mind?

Chapter Ten

Nicole parked the car and reached across the seat for the journal she'd brought with her to work that morning. Actually, it was more a book than a journal. She'd even named it.

Normally she didn't carry it around with her, but Remy had inspired so many new emotions and feelings that she'd felt compelled to put them to paper this morning. But when she'd tried to write, the words wouldn't come. Now they were echoing through her mind.

She'd never shared her journal with anyone, had never thought she would. But when Remy had asked about her life tonight, she'd found herself wanting to share the pain and the miracles with him.

What better way for him to really understand her than through the journal?

Before she changed her mind, she pulled a pen and note card from her purse. She jotted a quick message for Remy on the note card and then meticulously poured her heart into the journal.

When she finished, she hurried inside the apartment and set the bound journal and the note on the coffee table for him to find later.

Strangely it was Carlotta she thought of as she let herself out and took the elevator to the ground floor to hail a taxi. Carlotta had died, leaving a lover to search for her in vain. Nicole had lived, but no lover had ever come searching for her.

REMY WAS ALWAYS A BIT of an insomniac, but tonight was worse than usual. He'd slept an hour and then woken. Since then, he'd lain awake, alternately watching the shadows dance across the ceiling and the raindrops splatter against the windowpane.

He'd met with an FBI agent after he'd left Nicole and handed over the DVD. It was now in their hands. Still, he couldn't shake off the desire the parking-lot kiss had ignited. A mistake in every way, yet he couldn't get it or Nicole off his mind.

Finally he gave up, stretched his legs over the side of the bed and wiggled into his jeans. He zipped them enough to keep them from dropping to his ankles and went to the kitchen. The fridge was empty except for some condiments and a few bottles of beer.

He popped the top on a Shiner Bock and walked back to the small living area. Dropping to the sofa, he flicked on the lamp next to him and picked up a leather-bound journal. There was a note clipped to the cover.

You asked about my life, Remy. This is the condensed version. If you have time to read it, it may help you understand a bit more about who I am and what these past two days have meant to me. Nicole

Obviously she'd left it for him to read when she'd dropped off the car. He opened the binder. "Resurrection from Hell, a Journey of Survival" was written on the first page in perfect script. He turned to the next page and read the opening.

The person I had been died following Katrina. The person I'm becoming was born four days later when I was found, dehydrated, skin parched, my face beaten into a meaty, bloody pulp that had little resemblance to anything human.

So, like Carlotta, Remy and so many others, Nicole's life had been destroyed by the tragic hurricane and the flooding that followed. No wonder she hadn't wanted to talk about it last night.

The journal read like a novel, and Remy became so immersed in it, he didn't notice when the thunderstorm intensified and the raindrops became sheets of water.

Details flowed. The agony of waking up in a hospital and not knowing who or where she was. The hopelessness she'd felt when no one had come looking for her.

The despair when the police had told her that her fingerprints were not on file and her dental records were not a match to any-one reported missing after the storm.

When they'd removed the bandages and she'd gotten her first look at her pummeled face with its shattered bones and displaced features, she'd wanted to die. But then Leslie Cantrell had walked into her hospital room and offered her hope.

Dr. and Mrs. Cantrell wanted to give more than money to the victims of Katrina. They wanted to give of themselves. And give they did. With the blackness of amnesia still blocking all memories of past friends and family from Nicole's mind, Leslie offered her friendship and emotional support.

Dr. Cantrell offered his expertise. He performed surgery after surgery, all pro bono.

A nurse in the hospital dubbed the patient Nicole after a red-headed friend of hers. The name stuck.

When Nicole wasn't recovering in the hospital, she recovered in the Cantrells' home. They took her in and treated her like a daughter. To Nicole, they would forever be saints.

Thunder rattled the windows and lightning spiked the skies as Remy read the final pages. He was awed by Nicole's struggles and triumphs. She was truly amazing.

But she wasn't Carlotta.

She didn't have the innocence or the naïveté Carlotta had had back then. She'd lived through hell. But then, he wasn't the man he'd been eight years ago, either. Heartbreak had left him with an edge and a wariness that he hadn't possessed as a young cop who thought he had the world by the tail.

The time and date of the last notation in the diary indicated it had been written tonight—after the kiss. Remy read it hesi-tantly, not knowing what to expect after his blunder with the names.

For the first time since Katrina, I feel as if my heart is beginning to heal. Today, real excitement bubbled inside me. I took risks. I trusted a man I barely knew. I felt truly alive. No matter what happens after this, my life is forever changed for the better.

Dr. and Leslie Cantrell brought me back from hell. Remy Comeaux has brought me back to the threshold of love.

Remy closed the journal and carefully laid it back on the table. The storm was kicking up something fierce. But the desire to see Nicole was far more intense.

He knew that going to her now would lead to their making love. He'd never backed down from a risk where his job was involved.

Maybe it was time he took another chance on love.

NICOLE WAS ALREADY slick with desire when Remy slid between the sheets and joined her in her bed. When his lips took hers, she lost all inhibition. She responded hungrily, her tongue parrying with his, the thrill stealing her breath.

She'd waited so long for this kind of passion, had feared she'd never know the ecstasy of making love. But now Remy was here and she wanted him. Oh, how she wanted him.

His mouth moved to her breasts. He sucked each nipple in turn while his hand splayed her abdomen. Slowly his fingers trailed lower until they began to explore her most intimate places. She moaned and thrust against him.

"Take me. Please make love to me all the way."

He spread her legs then thrust his erection deep inside her. Over and over until the hot core inside her exploded.

"Oh, Remy."

"No, Nicole. It's not Remy."

She jerked awake. A flash of lightning lit the room like neon. Lee Barnaby was standing over her bed.

Chapter Eleven

Nicole's insides quaked and nausea merged with dread. "What are you doing here?"

"About to give you what you're begging for. Only it will be me instead of Remy inside you. Time you had a real man."

"No. We're friends, Lee. Please. Don't make it be like this."

"Friends don't conspire with a man's worst nemesis."

"If you're referring to Remy, you're wrong. I didn't conspire with him. I stayed away from him, just as you ordered me to do."

"You're a lying bitch, but you should have listened to me. Then you wouldn't have to die."

She jumped from the bed and tried to run. He grabbed her and threw her back to the bed. He held her arm behind her back with one hand while he unzipped his jeans with the other.

Lee truly was a monster, but she wouldn't give up. She couldn't. She'd gone through hell to get here. She couldn't die now.

"I knew the moment you saw Remy it would all be over."

"Nothing's over between us, Lee. Why would seeing Remy make anything over between us?"

He shoved a fist into her stomach. "No more lies, *Carlotta.* You'll take all the fun out of this for me."

Carlotta? Was Lee totally losing it? Was…

No. She had to be wrong. Even Lee couldn't have been that heartless. But she knew that he could.

Images attacked her mind in no apparent order, like flashbacks from someone else's life. If they were her memories, the timing couldn't be worse. A day ago they might have saved her life. But now they wouldn't let up. The doctor had said it might take a shock to trigger them.

"I'm Carlotta Worthington, aren't I?"

"If you say so."

"I am, and you knew it all along from my fingerprints. But why? Why keep my identity a secret?"

"You're a smart woman. Figure it out. Remy was working with the FBI to take me down. He would have, had it not been for Katrina."

"So you didn't tell him I'd been found as a way of getting back at him?"

"And it worked—until now."

"You're despicable."

Lee slapped her hard across the face and started to climb on top of her.

She stretched and wound her fingers around the bedside lamp. While he shoved down his boxers, she got in one swing at him, hitting the top of his head with the metal base.

He jerked back, stunned by the blow. She brought a knee to his crotch and took off running while he writhed in pain. She made it to the back door before he tackled her from behind, grabbing her ankles and yanking her to the floor.

That was when she saw the gun.

"You can't shoot me and get away with this, Lee. Your career will be over."

"My career was over the second you and Remy handed that film and my checkbooks over to the FBI."

"But we haven't. I promise. Remy still has them. Please let me go and I'll get them for you."

"I don't need your help. If Remy still has the video, I'll get it from him. Then neither of you will ever be seen again. Just two lovers who disappeared together to start their lives all over again somewhere far from the town where they'd suffered such heartbreak. It's a lovely story, really."

She had to keep him talking. If he pulled that trigger it would all be over. Just when she'd found out the truth about her identity. Just when her memories were starting to return.

Just when she had a chance to be with Remy, the love of her life.

"And if the video is already with the FBI?" she asked. "Then what?"

"Then I escape and retire in the Islands, somewhere even the FBI can't track me down."

Lee had it all worked out. He had no conscience. He was corrupt to the core and he was about to get away with murder again.

"You might kill me, Lee, but you'll never kill Remy. He'll take you down, just like he told you he would."

She tried to push away from him, but she was no match for his strength. When the pistol's barrel pushed against her head, she closed her eyes and screamed.

NICOLE WOULD PROBABLY think him crazy for showing up in the middle of a storm at 5:00 a.m. So be it. Remy turned onto her block. A second later his anticipation turned to a cold, choking knot in his stomach.

That was his pickup parked in her driveway. He'd know it anywhere. But Nicole wouldn't have driven it home. She couldn't have known where he'd parked it. She didn't have the key. She'd said she'd take a taxi.

Barnaby must have located his truck, or else someone had been following him when he'd parked it in the Quarter and walked to the apartment. He punched Redial on his phone, contacting the FBI agent he'd met with last night, to request emergency backup as he swerved into Nicole's driveway. Gun in hand, he jumped out of her car and raced to her front door.

A chilling scream punctuated a clap of thunder. The lock had already been pried open, so he turned the knob and rushed inside.

"Scream all you want. No one will hear you in this storm."

Remy paused at Lee's voice and backed against the wall, his finger on the trigger.

"Don't shoot me. Please don't shoot me. I can talk Remy into giving up the film. I know I can."

Nicole was pleading for her life. Damn Lee. Damn him to hell and back. Remy's muscles strained to storm in there and put a bullet in his head. But he couldn't act on instinct alone.

He had to play this smart. He couldn't risk Nicole's life.

"I wouldn't dream of shooting you, sweetheart—unless you force me, of course. Bullet wounds to the head are much too messy to clean up. We'll go back to the bedroom, this time for a date with your pillow. No ligature marks. No blood. Just a nice, fast suffocation. See, I'm more humane than you give me credit for."

Remy stayed out of sight, but he saw the gun at Nicole's head as Lee led her to the bedroom. He'd have to time this perfectly, judge when both of Lee's hands were off the gun and on the pillow before he made his move.

"Shoot me, you bastard. Clean up your dirty mess yourself for a change."

Remy's heart almost stopped completely as he heard Nicole's taunt, forcing Lee's hand.

He reached the doorway just as Lee raised a fist to strike her.

Nicole saw Remy. She gave one hard kick and the gun went flying from Lee's hand. His fist was in midswing.

"Hit her and you're a dead man."

Lee turned a ghostly shade of white and then made a dash for the back door. Remy started to give chase, but stopped when he spotted an armed FBI agent he remembered from eight years ago outside the kitchen window. He heard the squeal of brakes as more reinforcements arrived. They could handle the chief's arrest.

Nicole grabbed her heart as if holding it inside her chest. "Remy. Where on earth did you come from? How did you know Lee was here?"

"I didn't. For once, luck cut the deck my way."

"I'm Carlotta," she said. "Your Carlotta. Lee told me. He knew it all along. And now I remember you. From before. When we were falling in love."

He held her close. "I think you may be delirious, but you don't have to be Carlotta. Not for me. Not now."

"But I am. I know it sounds bizarre, but truly I am. Only, I think part of me is still Nicole."

He was having a hard time buying this. But her being Carlotta would make sense of a few things. Like why he'd fallen in love with Nicole at first sight. Not that he'd admitted it then.

"I love you," he said. "Whoever you are, I love you."

"I love you, too, Remy. I always have, even when I didn't remember who it was I loved."

"There is one problem. If you're really Carlotta, you owe me a wedding."

"Is tomorrow too soon?"

"Not as long as our forever after can start right now."

* * * * *

RITA HERRON

BAYOU JEOPARDY

CAST OF CHARACTERS

Mack Rivet—He was a detective before Katrina but was arrested on false charges. Now he's back to claim his freedom and the wife and child he lost, nothing will stop him, except death.

Lily Landry Rivet—She thought she'd lost Mack in the floods and now has a new life with her son. Can she risk her son being exposed to the dangers of Mack's job?

Winston Mack Rivet—He wants to know the truth about why his father was framed.

Melvin Landry—Lily's father never thought Mack was good enough for Lily. Did he frame him to get him out of his daughter's life?

Mayor Barrow—He claims he's helping rebuild the city. But is he stealing money from the rebuilding funds?

Tate Manning—Landry's lawyer and right-hand man wants Lily for himself. What lengths would he go to in order to get Mack out of the way?

Remy Comeaux—Private detective and former NOPD narcotics detective.

Ray Storm—An FBI agent involved in investigating corruption in the NOPD before Hurricane Katrina.

To my beautiful and sweet daughter Elizabeth
who lives in New Orleans and loves it!

Chapter One

Eight years ago when Katrina hit New Orleans and turned the city inside out, Mack Rivet had lost everything. His job as a detective. The woman he loved.

And the little boy she had been carrying.

He slid onto his usual bar stool at the Gator Saloon, shaking rain off his jacket as he made himself at home. Outside, the monsoon continued.

Cars were flooding. The river rising. People frantically searching for backup generators in case they lost power.

The bartender, Cooter Willis, set a cold black-and-tan in front of him, and Mack nodded his thanks.

He sipped the beer, hoping the cold liquid would soothe his nerves. But that same soul-deep ache ate at him as the storm continued to rage. Every time it rained, the haunting memories returned. Half of New Orleans's residents probably shared them.

Images of Lily and their little boy flashed in his mind.

If his son had survived, he would be eight. Mack would be carrying him to Saints games, teaching him how to shuck oysters, taking him gator watching in his pirogue in the bayou.

And Lily…beautiful, sweet Lily. She'd been too good for a man like him, but that hadn't seemed to matter. If she'd lived, they'd be making love right now, maybe making a second baby.

He chugged the beer, then slammed the glass down on the bar.

Reading his mood, Cooter slid him another one.

He'd been nursing his wounds for so long he didn't know how to do anything else. Hiding out in bayou country while the city rebuilt itself.

Grieving.

And waiting for the chance to clear his name.

Eight years later, and he was no closer to that than the day

Lee Barnaby had him hauled to jail. But he had been doing his research, keeping an eye on all the players.

He turned his second beer up and drank, the stench of his conversation with Barnaby still eating at him.

He hated most that Lily had died believing he was on the take.

"You're just like your old man," Barnaby had said. "You'll die in prison, too."

Hell, his father might have been dirty. But Mack had worked hard to stay on the up-and-up.

It hadn't mattered, though.

Sure, there had been corruption in the NOPD. The feds had known it and had enlisted him and his best friend, Remy Comeaux, into helping Special Agent Ray Storm with the investigation. The task force had been close to breaking that corruption wide open when Katrina hit.

Then all their lives had gone to hell.

He and Remy had been arrested. Ray transferred to God knew where.

The bar grew noisy as Friday night patrons filed in, and Cooter flipped on the TV.

A special news report suddenly interrupted the commercial, and a photograph of the very man he hated flashed on the screen. Lee Barnaby.

In handcuffs.

What the hell?

"In a shocking twist tonight, our city's chief of police, Lee Barnaby, has been arrested on charges of corruption as well as assault and attempted murder." The camera flashed onto Barnaby, who ducked his head, obviously trying to avoid being seen on camera.

"Private detective Remy Comeaux, who was once part of the NOPD himself, not only found evidence of drug trafficking, but apparently he saved Carlotta Worthington's life when Mr. Barnaby allegedly assaulted her." The reporter took a breath, then continued, "NOPD officer Doyle Shriver was killed when he became suspicious, leading to Lee Barnaby's arrest on corruption, tampering with evidence and the far more heinous crimes of the attempted murder of Carlotta Worthington. At this point, detectives believe they are just beginning to uncover the truth as to Mr. Barnaby's criminal activity. A full investigation is now under way."

Mack's pulse hammered. Remy had phoned him a couple of times this past week, but he hadn't taken the call. He hadn't known why Remy was back.

Did he wonder if Remy and Ray believed he was dirty?

Suddenly the beer burned like acid in his belly. He motioned to Cooter to get him a shrimp po'boy so he could sober up.

If Remy proved Barnaby was dirty, maybe Mack could prove Barnaby had set him up. It wouldn't bring back his wife and son, but clearing his name would be something.

LILY LANDRY RIVET LEANED over to kiss her son good-night, her heart swelling with love. He might have been born on the worst night in the history of New Orleans, but he was the best thing that had ever happened to her.

And every time she looked at him, she saw Mack Rivet, his father.

They shared the same coal-black hair, the same soul-deep brown eyes and the same bad-boy attitude.

It was a damn shame Mack hadn't gotten to know him.

Winston gave her a surly look as if he knew it was bedtime but he wasn't ready, and she almost laughed.

Maybe it was better he hadn't known his father. Especially after what she'd learned the night of Katrina...

"Do you have to go tonight, Mom?" Winston asked.

Lily ruffled his hair. "I told Grandpa I would, honey. But if you need anything, Anita will be here."

"I'm too old for a babysitter," Winston said with a pout.

"Anita is Grandpa's cook and maid and part of the family," Lily said. "So be nice to her."

Lily kissed him again. "Ten more minutes, then get some sleep. We'll go to the parade tomorrow."

His eyes lit up, and he crawled into bed with his computer. One of his favorite parts of living in New Orleans was the parades. And Mardi Gras had been an exciting experience.

The kid was obsessed with alligators, too.

She left the room, then grabbed her shawl.

She'd agreed to accompany her father to help him with the fundraiser. Gerard Barrow had been the deputy director of the Louisiana Disaster Avoidance Task Force, LDAT, before Katrina. Since the flooding, he'd worked hard to rebuild the city. Her father had been his right-hand man, and she had joined the efforts.

She checked her lipstick in the mirror then descended the steps. Her father was waiting with his driver. He ushered her into the limo, and they headed toward the Quarter.

But loneliness settled into her as they drove down Saint Charles Avenue, and she fingered the emerald stone at her neck. It was smaller than the expensive jewelry her father had given her, but Mack had bought it for her the night after they'd first made love, and she hadn't been able to let go of it.

Even after NOPD officer Charles Gibbons had shown her proof that Mack was a dirty cop and that he had been cheating on her.

MACK PULLED HIS JACKET up to keep the rain from soaking his neck as he went to meet Remy.

A limo rolled by, spewing rain all over him, and he cursed. Damn rich people thought they owned the world. Maybe that had been Barnaby's problem. He'd wanted to be one of them.

Mack never had. Never would.

Even if he had wanted it, he wouldn't have fit. Lily's father had pointed that out repeatedly.

He ducked beneath an awning. The rain had finally stopped, but water stood in the alleys, dripping from the storefronts. A half-dozen patrons strolled in and out of the bars, and tourists rushed by. A man and woman holding hands caught his eye as they stopped to window-shop at the jewelry store where he'd bought Lily an emerald, and his gut tightened.

But the sight of Remy Comeaux with his Saints hat on jerked Mack back to his mission. Remy visually searched the area.

Maybe he was worried about repercussions from Barnaby's arrest.

If Barnaby had cronies working for him, they might seek revenge against Remy.

Mack walked toward him, his gaze tracking the area in case he was walking into a trap.

Once a cop, always a cop.

"Long time." Remy gestured toward the fence behind them. "Last time I saw you we were leaving that jail."

Mack chuckled. "Yeah, I heard your papers got lost."

"Yours probably did, too," Remy said.

"That doesn't mean that my name is clear."

Remy nodded. "Barnaby's in jail. That's a start. But he's just a small part of this game."

"Go on."

"Like Ray said eight years ago, the corruption runs about as deep and wide as Lake Pontchartrain."

Mack shoved his hands in his pockets. "Any evidence?"

"Suspicions ranging from police corruption to financial plans for the city's rebuilding efforts to politics."

"You're talking about the mayor?" Mack asked.

"Yeah, maybe even higher."

Remy removed a file from inside his jacket and handed it to him. "Look over that and see what you think."

Mack opened the file. Charles Gibbons's name was scrawled there, although Remy had made a note that Gibbons had led Remy to a drug dealer connected to Barnaby, so Gibbons was an ally.

Mayor Barrow was on the list. So was Melvin Landry.

His mind raced.

Landry had money and was buddies with Barrow. If there was corruption with the rebuilding funds, Barrow and Landry might be involved.

Suspicions rose. Landry had disliked him, hadn't wanted him to marry his precious daughter, Lily.

Had Landry framed him to get him away from his daughter?

"What do you think?" Remy asked. "Are you in?"

Mack's gaze met Remy's. "You want me to work with you? I thought—"

"That I believed the charges against you?" Remy's low chuckle rumbled. "Did you believe them about me?"

Mack shook his head. "Not for a damn minute."

A smile creased his friend's face. "Me, neither."

Emotions Mack hadn't felt in a long time hit him. "Oh, yeah, I'm in. If Lily's father set me up, I'll nail him."

Remy pushed another piece of paper into his hand. "Landry's at a dinner with the mayor now at this restaurant."

He and Remy agreed to keep in touch, and Mack walked toward the restaurant, a pricey two-story establishment. The rain began to drizzle again, the sky dark with more clouds.

All he could think about was the fact that he might finally find out who'd ruined his reputation and sent him to jail on trumped-up charges.

He stopped across the street from the place, the sounds of Bourbon Street echoing with partiers.

He people watched for a while, listening to the rhythmic blues and zydeco music, then finally the dinner party spilled onto the veranda overlooking the city.

Mayor Barrow. His wife, Genita. Three other men he didn't recognize.

Then Melvin Landry strode outside, a glass of champagne in his hand, a woman on his arm.

Mack squinted through the rain to see who was with him, but shadows hid the woman's face. Still, she had blond hair piled on top of her head, blond hair that reminded him so much of Lily that his throat closed.

She said something to Landry, walked to the edge of the veranda and looked out over the Quarter, a sliver of streetlight catching her face.

Mack staggered backward.

Dear God. It was Lily.

Chapter Two

Shock and disbelief slammed into Mack. He couldn't believe Lily was alive.

His hand trembled as he wiped sweat from his brow. Why had her father told him she was dead?

Bile rose to his throat.

First Landry had him thrown in jail on false charges, then he must have been furious when Mack survived the flooding prison.

And when he'd come looking for Lily—hell. He'd probably figured telling him Lily was dead would be the end of him.

And it nearly had been. He'd sulked away to grieve just as Landry had predicted.

God. What about the baby? Had he survived?

Did he have a son?

He balled his hands into fists. Did Lily know he'd made it out of that jail?

Was she aware her father might be stealing money from the funds they'd raised to help the city?

Too agitated to stand still, he began to pace. Rainwater squished between his shoes, the sounds of Bourbon Street fading as his anger took root.

Dammit. He wanted to nail Landry.

But first, he'd watch Lily. If she'd known he was alive, why hadn't she tried to find him?

LILY SENSED SOMEONE watching her from the veranda and scanned the street below. A figure moved to the right and ducked into a bar, and she chided herself for being paranoid.

Ever since she'd moved back to New Orleans, she'd seen Mack in the shadows, Mack in the streets, Mack waiting on her at their favorite coffee shop with a latte.

But Mack was gone.

The jail where he was had flooded. Some of the prisoners had escaped, and although Mack's body hadn't been recovered, the fact that he hadn't come looking for her made her certain he'd died in the floods.

She turned to her father. "I'm tired, Dad. I'm going to take a cab home. I'll pick up Winston in the morning."

Her father frowned. "I thought you might spend the night tonight."

How could she explain to him that she needed to be alone? "Maybe next time." She went to say good-night to the mayor. Piano music played softly in the background, champagne floated freely through the room.

Mayor Barrow squeezed her hand. "Thank you for all you're doing for our city. The fundraisers you've organized have raised hundreds of thousands of dollars already."

"I just want everyone who lost their homes to have one again."

He nodded, and she said good-night to the investors. Then she retrieved her wrap and headed down the stairs. The maître d' called her a cab, and within minutes, she was slipping inside her house on Saint Charles Street.

Darkness bathed the inside, and she reached for the lamp, but suddenly someone grabbed her from behind.

She tried to scream, but he shoved a hand over her mouth and pushed her toward the den.

"I'm not going to hurt you," he murmured in her ear.

His voice sounded vaguely familiar, yet fear seized her. If he wasn't going to hurt her, why had he broken in?

Prepared to offer him her purse and whatever else he wanted in the house, she nodded against his hand.

He eased her toward the sofa, then flipped on the lamp, and she spun around, ready to tangle.

But her heart stalled in her chest. Her attacker was Mack Rivet.

Her former lover and husband. And the father of her son.

MACK'S HEART POUNDED so hard that he had to take a deep breath to calm himself. He thought he'd lost Lily years ago, and now here she was alive, in the flesh.

And looking like a knockout in that skintight black sheath.

Just touching her stirred a deep ache in his soul.

And in his groin.

Her long blond hair was captured in a chignon with jewel combs holding the silky strands in place.

A reminder that her father had money and that she was too good for him.

Still, it hadn't stopped him from wanting her—and having her—eight years ago.

It wouldn't stop him now.

"Oh, my God," Lily said in a choked whisper. "I thought… you died in the flood."

"No." Mack narrowed his eyes at her. "But I thought you were dead."

Emotions flickered in her eyes. "You looked for me?"

"Of course I did," he said with a muttered curse. "Dammit, I loved you, Lily. You were pregnant with my son."

Lily paled. "I don't understand. It's been years."

"I know it has," he said sharply.

She raised her gaze to his, those damn emerald eyes drawing him in. "Father said he checked the listings and a guard said you died."

Anger gnawed at Mack. Landry had lied to both of them.

Which made him even more certain that he was aiding the mayor in his scheme.

"Why did you wait eight years to come to me?" she asked.

Mack's defenses rose as she turned the tables on him. "I did look for you, for months," he said, his heart in his throat. "I kept checking the lists, the police departments and hospitals, and I called your father, but he told me you didn't make it."

Lily gasped and sank onto the sofa. "What… No…" She knotted her hands in her lap. "Why would my father say that?"

"You tell me." Mack gritted his teeth as he realized her father had gotten what he'd wanted—he'd torn them apart.

Denial flickered in her eyes. "It has to be a mistake. Maybe he checked and couldn't find out anything about you so he made up that story."

"He spoke to me, so he knew I was alive. And he told me that you were gone, and obviously he knew you weren't," Mack said.

Lily frowned. "You were watching me tonight?"

"I was watching your father and the mayor," Mack said. "Then I saw you on the veranda and was shocked to discover you'd survived."

Lily dropped her head into her hands.

His chest squeezed. For the life of him, he wanted to believe that she had no part in her father's or Barrow's illegal actions.

But dammit, she had believed the worst of him. That still hurt.

"Where have you been?" she asked in a pained whisper.

"Living in the bayou, helping other folks find missing loved ones. Trying to find evidence to clear my name from those bogus arrest charges." He didn't tell her that he suspected her father had set him up.

"The charges you believed, Lily."

Lily began to pull the combs from her hair as if she needed to do something with her hands. The silky strands fell around her shoulders, and she finger combed them, making his hands ache to do the same.

"That was because Lee Barnaby showed me proof," Lily said, her voice rising an octave. "He had documents, evidence that you were taking bribes and selling drugs."

Memories bombarded him. That night he'd been waiting on her call, worried she might go into labor.

Instead Lee Barnaby had slapped handcuffs on him and ruined his life.

"I know what you saw, Lily, but Barnaby fabricated all that evidence." He pressed a hand to his chest. "You know what happened to my father, how I grew up. I would never take a bribe or sell drugs."

Lily shot up from her seat. "What about that photo of you with your girlfriend, Mack? That looked pretty real to me."

"My girlfriend? What the hell are you talking about?"

"Angelica, the woman with the sultry body and chocolate eyes," Lily said. "I believe you call her Angel."

Another shock wave rolled through Mack. "Good God, Lily, you can't believe that I was cheating on you."

Her beautiful pouty lips formed a frown. "He showed me pictures of you with her, Mack. The two of you cozy in a dark bar, in an alley, in a car."

Mack hissed between his teeth. "Angelica was not my girlfriend. She was my C.I."

Lily stared at him, the tension stretching between them, war raging in her eyes.

"I was working undercover with a federal agent named Ray Storm. He had evidence against Barnaby that would have put him away for corruption and drug trafficking. Two years before that, I arrested Angelica for dealing. She was an addict, but I persuaded her to slip me information." He scraped a hand over his chin. "If we looked cozy, it was part of my undercover work, Lily. I swear it."

Lily's lower lip trembled. "You…really weren't with her?"

"Never," Mack said emphatically. "I loved you. And I did not accept any bribes."

"Oh God, Mack," Lily whispered. "I can't believe my father lied to me and that Barnaby set you up."

"His arrest should validate my story," Mack said. Although, getting Barnaby was only the beginning. There were others on the take, bigger fish to fry.

For the first time since he'd entered the place, Mack's gaze scanned the room. A second later, he saw what he was searching for. A photograph on the built-in bookshelves by the fireplace.

A photo of a little boy who looked so much like him that his throat swelled.

He picked it up, his heart pounding. The little boy had dark black hair like his, the same stubborn jaw and intense brown eyes. And that cowlick. Damn, he even had his cowlick.

Another photo of the boy caught his eye, this one with Landry at Christmas.

Anger at all the time he'd missed choked him. "Where is he? What's his name?"

Tears glittered on Lily's eyelashes. "Winston Mack Rivet. He's spending the night at my father's."

So she had named their son after him.

"I have to see him," he said, heading toward the door. "I've missed eight years of his life."

Lily ran after him and grabbed his arm. "Wait, Mack, you can't, not tonight."

He swung toward her, his jaw clamped tight. "Dammit, Lily, I thought you two were dead. I…thought I'd lost you, but you were both alive all along."

"I'm sorry, Mack." Lily's voice cracked. "I…I'm so sorry."

Mack was trembling. "What did you tell him about me?"

Lily blinked back more tears. "Just what I thought, that you died in the storm."

"Well, I'm not dead," he said. "And I want to see my son."

"You will," Lily said. "But he's sleeping now, Mack. We can't wake him up. Let's wait until the right time."

When would the right time be?

When he cleared his name? When he arrested Lily's father?

Dammit, he had to find out the truth, but if he had to arrest her father, Lily would hate him.

And so might his son.

Chapter Three

Mack reined in his temper. She was right. It would be a shock for Winston to learn his father was alive. No use doing it in the middle of the night. "How about in the morning? I'll go with you to pick him up at your father's."

Lily rubbed her arms, her face panicked. "I'm not sure that's such a good idea, Mack. Especially considering the trouble between you and my father."

"He lied to us both," Mack said. "He owes us an explanation."

Lily flinched. "I'm sorry, Mack."

"Stop apologizing for him," Mack said. "It's your father who should be sorry. He never wanted us to be together, and by lying he got his wish."

"Mack—"

"It's true and you know it." Mack inhaled a calming breath, questions bombarding him. "What happened that night, Lily? Where have you and Winston been all these years?" God, was she involved with someone else?

Lily sighed. "The night of the storm, I went into labor. Daddy's friend flew me to Alabama in his helicopter before the worst hit. I gave birth to Winston that night, and we lived there until a couple of months ago." She rubbed a hand over her mouth, drawing him to those damned kissable lips. "Meanwhile, Dad was working with Mayor Barrow on the rebuilding campaign, and he convinced me to move back and help."

Mack gestured to the house. "But you didn't move in with him?"

Lily smiled sardonically. "No, I wanted to be queen of my own castle."

Mack nodded. "You always did like having your own space."

And she had stood up to her father. At one time, he'd even wondered if she'd dated him as an act of rebellion.

Still, rebelling and helping him get dirt on her father were two different things.

"What time are you going to your father's house in the morning?"

Lily chewed her bottom lip. "Eight. I want to have breakfast with Winston."

Eight o'clock sounded like decades away. But he didn't want to frighten his son by storming in and attacking Landry.

Which was exactly what he might do if he saw him tonight.

"Mack?"

"Breakfast with our son sounds good." He paused. "And, Lily, don't tell your father I'm coming."

Her eyes darkened with worry, but she gave a short nod, and he left before he dragged her into his arms and reminded her that she was his wife.

But he couldn't push her.

Because he was afraid of what he might find—that she'd moved on without him.

He couldn't tell her that he was investigating her father, either. Not until he was sure about his facts.

He climbed into his Range Rover and started the engine. He couldn't wait to see the look on Melvin Landry's face when he realized he'd been caught in his lies.

And when he discovered that Mack was back in their lives.

THE NEXT MORNING Lily was ready to go by seven. She hadn't slept a wink for thinking about Mack. She opened her jewelry drawer, removed her wedding ring and rubbed her fingers over the silver band.

Mack had apologized for not giving her diamonds, but she hadn't cared. She'd been so in love with him she could barely breathe. She'd had diamonds from her father; she'd wanted romance and excitement from Mack. She'd thought his undercover work risky but had thrived on living on the wild side.

Now that she had a child, Lily wasn't sure she wanted to take those risks again. Or to worry about whether Mack would come home at night. Or if some dangerous criminal might attack her or Winston to get revenge against him.

For eight years, she'd grieved for him, had told Winston stories about how tough his father had been. That he'd saved lives and protected innocents.

Even though she'd wondered about the charges against him.

And now here he was alive, claiming he'd been framed, and he wanted to meet his son.

Why had her father lied to her? And why had he told Mack she was dead?

Because Mack was right. Her father had never wanted them to be together.

Fresh tears blurred her eyes, but she blinked them away. She had to rely on her anger this morning to face her father.

A knock sounded on the door, and she checked the peephole. Just as she'd expected, Mack stood on the stoop. A sight she'd craved for so long that her knees nearly buckled.

Last night he'd looked like a renegade, his hair shaggy, his beard a few days old and his clothes wrinkled, as if he'd slept in them for days.

Today he looked freshly shaven, his hair trimmed, and he wore clean jeans and a white collared shirt.

Her body hummed with arousal. Part of her wanted to haul him to bed and remind him how much she'd loved him.

But she had to think of her son. Technically Mack still needed to clear his name.

Her palms were sweating as she opened the door. Mack shifted, looking nervous. That small display made her heart throb with affection.

And anger at her dad for keeping them apart. Winston deserved to know his father.

"Are you ready?" he asked.

She nodded. "I'll drive my car, though. I'll need it later."

Mack frowned but agreed, and he followed her to her father's estate. They walked to the door together, the mood tense as Lily rang the doorbell.

Anita answered. "Why, Miss Lily, what are you doing knocking?"

Lily gestured toward Mack. "I brought someone with me. I thought it might be best. Would you tell Daddy to meet me in the study?"

Anita nodded. "Of course, dear." Anita escorted them to her father's office and gestured toward the coffeepot. "Help yourselves."

"Where's Winston?" Lily asked.

"At the batting cage. Do you want me to get him?"

"Not yet. Just tell Daddy I'm here."

Anita nodded then disappeared, and Mack released a pent-up breath.

Lily wondered how she would feel if she was in his shoes. Eight long years of thinking his son had died and Mack was about to meet him.

Mack drummed his fingers on her father's desk. "A batting cage?"

"Dad had one built for Winston last year when he joined the school baseball team."

Another event Mack had missed.

She wanted to hear her father's reason for lying.

And she didn't intend to let him off the hook until she got some answers.

DAMMIT. MACK HAD ALREADY missed so much of his son's life. And Landry was obviously buying his son with batting cages and no telling what other kinds of expensive gifts that he couldn't afford on a cop's salary.

Hell, he didn't even have a steady income now.

Lily fidgeted while he studied the photos on the wall. Winston when he was a baby in a red wagon. Winston at one of the Mardi Gras parades. Winston with Landry at a Saints game.

Once again, the ache of what he'd missed gnawed at his insides. If Landry hadn't lied to him, that would have been a photograph of him and his son at the game.

The opposite wall held pictures of Landry with Barnaby and

the mayor. Another one of Landry with Martin Hennessey, a former real-estate mogul, now a gubernatorial candidate. There were also framed newspaper stories of Landry's personal contributions to the building fund as well as elaborate fundraisers and parties he'd hosted.

Questions about Landry's and the mayor's possible illegal handling of funds nagged at him. He needed access to Landry's computer to search for answers.

But Landry wouldn't willingly hand that over. And if he asked, he'd tip his hand that he was investigating the mayor.

Mack inched closer to Landry's computer, hoping for the right opportunity, but he couldn't get to it with Lily in the room. Still, he removed a tiny camera from his pocket, pretended to adjust one of the pictures on the wall and placed it at the edge of the frame.

"I've been thinking, Mack. Maybe we shouldn't introduce you to Winston yet."

Mack folded his arms. "Why the hell not?"

"It just might be better if I told him about you first, then we set up a meeting."

"Lily, I've waited eight years to see him. I'm not waiting another damn day."

The office door opened then and Landry stepped inside. Tiny age lines fanned the corners of the man's mouth, and silver tipped the edges of his hair.

But his cold gray eyes hadn't changed. They were still fierce and formidable.

Landry muttered a curse when he saw Mack. "So you finally crawled out from under the rock where you've been hiding."

"Yeah, and look who I found," Mack said through clenched teeth. "Imagine my surprise. Lily and my son didn't die in the storm like you said." He stepped closer to Landry, his hands curled into fists. "Then again, you knew that all along."

Landry poured himself a cup of coffee then gestured toward Lily.

She shook her head no. "Why did you tell him Winston and I died?"

"Because a father's job is to protect his child."

"I didn't need your protection, Dad," Lily cried. "I deserved the truth. And my son needed a father but you denied him that."

"Yes, Winston needed a father but not a criminal for one." Landry's expression turned chilling. "When the storm hit, Rivet, you had just been arrested. You may have escaped in the storm, but that simply makes you a fugitive like half the other lowlifes the state lost during Katrina."

Mack gritted his teeth. "Then why didn't you send someone after me when I called you about Lily?"

Landry sipped his coffee. "I figured the police would catch you sooner or later."

Mack arched a brow. "As long as I wasn't bothering your daughter, you were fine to let me go free?"

"I'm not fine with anyone who breaks the law," Landry said harshly.

Mack barely controlled his rage. "But you're okay framing an innocent man?"

"If you're as innocent as you claim, why have you been hiding out?" Landry asked. "Why didn't you face the charges like a man?"

"Because I was set up." Mack's voice rose. "And I think you helped frame me."

A noise sounded and Mack looked up to see Winston standing in the doorway, a shocked expression on his face.

Dear God, he'd wanted to meet his son. But he didn't want him to hear him and Landry hurling accusations at each other.

TEARS BURNED LILY'S EYES at the pained look on her son's face. Good Lord. This was not the way she wanted to introduce him to Mack. She should have told Anita to make sure he stayed outside.

Winston stared up at Mack. "You're my father?"

Mack took a deep breath. "Yes, I am, son."

Winston glanced back and forth between them. "Why did you all lie to me?"

"Honey, I can explain," Lily said. Had her father really believed Mack was guilty of the crimes he'd been accused of?

She had....

"I'm sorry, Winston," Mack said. "I... There was a terrible misunderstanding and I thought you and your mother were gone."

"We're not," Winston said with a stubborn lift to his chin. "And Mom cried at night for you, but you never came."

Then he turned and ran from the room.

Lily hated to leave Mack alone with her father.

But she had to talk to her son, so she left them together.

MACK GLARED AT LANDRY. "Do you really think it was good for my little boy to believe his father was dead when he needed me?"

Landry shot him a lethal look. "If his father is a dirty cop, yes. With me, that boy has a chance at a good life. He'll attend the best schools, camps, sports activities, anything he wants. That's what I can give him." Landry's voice hardened. "What do you have to offer? You're broke and are facing criminal charges. You know what it was like growing up under the shadow of your own father's incarceration. Do you want that for Winston?"

Mack's gut tightened. Landry knew how to play hardball.

He'd hated the taunts other kids had thrown at him. Had hated being a jailbird kid.

His mother had died heartbroken and humiliated.

Landry cleared his throat. "If you have any feelings toward Winston, you'll leave him and Lily alone."

That would be the unselfish thing to do.

But his son's face flashed in Mack's mind. If anything, he had to prove his innocence now for Winston.

"You have a point," Mack said. "But the thing you're missing is that I'm innocent, Landry. And I intend to prove it."

Chapter Four

Mack called Remy as soon as he left Landry's and filled him in.

"You mean he lied to you?" Remy asked.

"He sure as hell did. He and Barnaby and the mayor are tight, too. Makes me wonder if he enlisted Barnaby to frame me."

"Son of a bitch," Remy said. "So what are you going to do?"

"Prove I'm innocent."

"If Landry is working for the mayor, they might both be misusing the rebuilding funds."

"I'll try to access his files on Lily's computer and check his financials."

"Sounds good."

"Whatever happened to Angelica?"

Remy chuckled. "Hell, you haven't heard? She's a narc now."

"Wonders never cease," Mack said. "How can I contact her?"

"On the streets, just like always."

Mack thanked him then hung up. But he couldn't stop thinking about Landry.

Or Lily and his son.

A pang shot through him. Winston looked so much like him. If only he hadn't overheard the confrontation between his father and his grandfather.

Part of him wanted Landry to be guilty so he could arrest him. But putting him in jail would hurt Lily.

And his son.

Winston had probably been snowed by Landry's money.

The very thought galled Mack. He wanted his child to learn values, that you had to work hard to get what you wanted, that it wasn't handed to you on a silver platter.

God knew nothing had ever come easy to him.

Except police work. Playing the underbelly came naturally.

So did living in the bayou.

What would Winston and Lily think about the hole-in-the-wall where he kept residence?

Hell, he'd cross that bridge when he came to it.

Right now he needed to clear his name.

So he headed back to Lily's. She would probably be with Winston and her father for a while.

It was the perfect time to look at her computer.

And if he didn't find anything to help him in her files, he'd find a way to hack into Landry's.

LILY KNOCKED ON THE DOOR to the guest room her father had had designed for Winston. The room was decorated with sports memorabilia that her father had thought would impress Winston.

But neither she nor her dad had been able to be the substitute father Winston needed.

No one had filled that spot. But Mack was back, and he wanted that role.

How could she deny either of them that?

She knocked again and heard a muffled response, so she opened the door and stepped inside.

Her son was sprawled facedown on the bed. Her heart squeezed. He tried so hard to be the man of the house.

No eight-year-old should shoulder that responsibility.

"Winston," she said softly as she walked toward the bed, "I know you're upset."

He sniffled then swiped at the tears he didn't want her to see.

"We have to talk," Lily said softly.

He rolled over, his red, puffy eyes breaking her heart.

"You and Grandpa knew he was alive and you didn't tell me."

A mountain of pain echoed in his words. She was his mother; she had to soothe the hurt.

She sat down beside him. "Listen to me, Winston. I love you and I have never lied to you."

"But—"

She placed a hand on his cheek. "I didn't lie. I thought we lost your father during the hurricane."

Winston scrubbed a fist across his eyes. Eyes that looked so much like Mack's that her heart clenched. Her little boy had lost so much by not having his father around.

And he could have been around if her father hadn't lied to them. Even if he thought he'd had good reason, that should have been her decision, not his.

"But Grandpa—"

"He probably received some misinformation," she said, deciding to spare Winston. After all, her dad adored Winston and her son adored him.

Winston heaved a weary sigh. "So…is Dad bad like Grandpa said, or is he like you said?"

Lily stretched out beside her son and looked at the ceiling. It was painted white, unlike the glittering stars on the ceiling at their house, the ones she'd added because Winston commented that they reminded him of heaven, where he thought his father was.

No wonder he was confused.

"Honey," she said softly, "you don't understand the way it was when Katrina hit. The flooding, the levees breaking, the people trying to flee the city. It was mad chaos. Families were literally torn apart. The phones were down. Rescue workers had orders to only take the women and children. There were thousands of people shoved into shelters, into the Dome, people being transported to other cities." Her lungs squeezed for air as she recalled her water breaking, the labor pains, the terror of not knowing where Mack was.

"So many people lost their families and their homes back then. And the system failed, so learning what happened to friends and family was impossible."

"I know that," he said. "They talk about it at school, showed us pictures and stuff. What I want to know is if my daddy is the man you said." He looked at her with so much anguish and childlike hope that there was no way she could crush it.

"He was, he *is* the tough, honorable man I described," she said. She squeezed her son's hand.

Although, she had no idea what was going to happen between them now.

MACK HATED BREECHING Lily's trust by breaking into her house, but he couldn't confront her with suspicions about her father or the mayor.

Not and win her back.

She won't trust you when she finds out you're trying to incriminate her father.

But he had to clear his name for his son, so he picked the lock, stepped inside and shut the door, then scanned the foyer. The place was so quiet he could hear his breath escaping.

He wanted to see Winston's room.

Although a thought struck him.

He had been gone eight years. Lily had thought he was dead.

Was she involved with someone else?

The thought of another man touching her, making love to her, made his blood boil.

The thought of another man playing father to his son was even worse.

The soul-deep ache that had consumed him the past few years returned full force, nearly immobilizing him, but he tamped it down.

His wife and son were alive.

He would get them back.

Knowing Lily could return any minute, he crossed the foyer to the office. Then he removed the flash drive from his pocket and booted up her computer.

He spent the next few minutes copying all of her files.

Tonight he would go down to the Quarter and find Angelica. He wanted the skinny on Barnaby and his drug operation.

If anyone could help him, Angel could.

LILY FINALLY CONVINCED Winston to go downstairs to breakfast. Her father was unusually talkative, obviously striving to make up for the earlier confrontation.

Winston tried to rally, but he was still upset.

Even when the three of them went to the parade, he stood on the sidelines and didn't run for the candy and trinkets.

"Let's get beignets," her father suggested. Beignets were always Winston's favorites.

"I'm not hungry," Winston said. "I just want to go home."

Disappointment lined her father's face, but she couldn't blame Winston. She was still angry with her dad herself.

The ride back to her father's was steeped in tension, and when her dad suggested they stay so Winston could swim in the backyard pool, he declined.

"I don't feel good," he said, then rubbed his belly.

Lily didn't want to argue. Her son had had a rough day.

He needed time to process the fact that his father was alive.

So did she. Being alive meant Mack was back in their lives, whether she wanted it or not.

They drove to her house in silence, and when she unlocked the door, she inhaled Mack's scent and had the uneasy feeling that he was still there.

But when she combed through the rooms, they were empty.

Winston went to his room to play video games and she retreated to her office to work on the spring fundraiser.

But an uneasy feeling enveloped her. Lee Barnaby's arrest made her wonder if Mack was right. Barnaby could have had something to do with framing him.

But her father couldn't be involved.

He hadn't approved of Mack, but he wouldn't have done something so underhanded as to have him arrested on false charges.

Would he?

Mack dressed for work, his jeans with the holes in them, ratty T-shirt, dirty cap. If he wanted to fit in with the homeless and the junkies, he had to play the part.

He'd spent the afternoon studying Lily's files, although he hadn't found what he was looking for, just planning schedules and details on caterers, menus, silent-auction items, guests.

Nothing incriminating.

He needed to look at Landry's files. But getting access to his study would be impossible with his security and staff.

He wove through the French Quarter, keeping his head low

but alert as he mingled with the late-night crowd. He passed two kids tap-dancing with bottle tops glued to the bottoms of their shoes, their act drawing an audience, their tip bucket filling. Another trio sat playing jazz music on the corner.

Finally he spotted one of his former contacts sprawled in the corner, leaning against a run-down storefront, a brown bag in his hand.

Mack squatted beside him. "Same corner, I see."

Buddy nodded. He was a war vet who'd lost the lower half of his right leg in combat. When he returned to the States, his life had fallen apart.

"What are you doing back?" Buddy mumbled. "Heard you bit the dust."

He had felt dead the past few years. "Not dead, and I'm back, looking for Angelica."

Buddy's eyebrows rose. "She's working the strip club around the corner."

He'd heard she was a narc. Must be staking the joint. "You'll have to be more specific."

Buddy grinned, his silver tooth shining. "The Bare Babes."

Mack stuffed a few bills in Buddy's hands. "Get a decent meal."

Buddy laughed and sipped his booze.

Mack stood and headed to the strip club. Loud rock music blared from speakers, and a scantily clad girl with fake boobs waved to passersby, coaxing them inside. Mack winced at the cheap strobe light flashing across the interior. Two half-naked girls pole danced in the middle of the room.

Neither was Angelica. She stood behind the bar, swirling drinks, her café au lait skin gleaming beneath the dim bar lighting. A hint of surprise lit her eyes when she spotted him, but neither gave away that they knew each other. Instead, he feigned interest in the strippers, then claimed a bar stool.

She waited on two already half-drunk men, then sashayed over to him.

"I knew that flood didn't get you. Nothing going to kill a swamp devil like you."

A smile twitched on his mouth, and he sipped the beer she'd set in front of him. "Looking to clear my name. Comeaux thinks Barnaby was only a peon compared to the corruption in the city."

"Who are you looking at?"

"Melvin Landry. Mayor Barrow."

She whistled, the tassels on her top twirling. "Going after your father-in-law. That takes guts."

"Or stupidity."

She nodded and wiped the counter, her gaze cutting around the room. "I think Remy might be right."

"What have you heard?"

"Someone paid to get rid of you and him. Don't imagine they're going to be happy to have you back."

Especially now the players had risen in ranks. Barnaby had moved up to chief of police and Hennessey was running for governor.

"Too bad for them," he said. "Got any tips?"

She lowered her voice. "Barrow likes to spend money on his women."

"You mean hookers?"

She gave a quick nod. "Has a couple of regulars."

Mack wondered who paid for that. "Word on the street is that he was supposed to have rebuilt the businesses three streets over, but he keeps stalling."

"Because he's filling his own pockets with cash and buying diamonds and condos for his girls."

Made sense. "I need a hacker to get into Landry's files. If they're skimming money from the rebuilding fund, I need proof."

Another customer flagged Angelica for a drink. She served him a whiskey, then handed drafts to two more customers. When she returned, she slid a napkin in front of him. Like a pro, she'd scrawled a name and phone number on it.

"Tell him I sent you."

He folded the napkin and tucked it into his pocket. "Thanks. Be careful, Angel."

"You're the one who should be careful." She took his empty

mug. "If they wanted you gone eight years ago, think how they'll react now with you asking questions."

She was right, but he wasn't going away. He had to prove something to his son.

He walked through the Quarter, then made it to his car. He was just about to get in it when a shot rang out.

Mack ducked as the bullet sailed by his head and shattered his back windshield.

Chapter Five

Mack ducked to avoid taking a bullet, quickly scanning the area for the shooter. But the noise from Bourbon Street made it impossible to know where the bullet had come from.

He reached for his gun, keeping it out of sight from tourists as he searched the area.

A carriage rolled by carrying a couple of lovebirds, while other patrons wove in and out of the bars.

He kept low, using his hand to rake glass off his seat before he slipped inside his SUV. He didn't see the shooter, but he kept his eyes peeled. A man painted in all silver drew a crowd to the left of him.

A black sedan sped past him, the windows tinted.

Was the shooter in that car?

Or was he on the street hiding in the crowd?

Dammit, the area was so packed that he could have easily hidden or already disappeared.

Mack sat for another few minutes, then started the engine and left the Quarter, wondering who in the hell had shot at him. He'd pissed off a lot of people years ago, but hardly anyone knew he was in town again.

Except for Landry.

Would his father-in-law actually hire someone to shoot him in order to keep him away from Lily?

His back windshield was shattered, but it was too late now to get it repaired. He'd take it to the shop tomorrow. He pulled over at a gas station, grabbed his flashlight from the dash and searched for the bullet casing.

It took him a minute to spot it, but he dug it from the back of his seat and examined it. A .38. He retrieved a Baggie from the dash and stored it to send to the lab.

Did Landry own a .38?

He glanced at the number Angelica had written on the napkin, memorized it, then punched it into his cell phone.

The phone rang three times, then a male voice answered. "This is Einstein."

"Angel gave me your name. I want to hire you."

"For what?"

"A job."

"What kind of job?"

"One that requires discretion."

"What makes you think I can help?"

"Our mutual friend says you're the best." Might as well make the guy feel wanted.

"How do I know you're not a cop?"

Mack bit back a laugh. "I was a cop a few years ago. That's how I met Angel. But I'm not on the force now."

"How come?"

"Some dirty cop framed me for a crime I didn't do. Trying to clean up the mess."

A hesitant pause, then Einstein mumbled an okay. "I do this and there's no repercussions? You don't get your badge back then come after me?"

"No one will know about our arrangement but us. You have my word."

The young man gave him an address in Terrytown.

Mack drove back onto the interstate, bypassed the Dome, then took the exit to the West Bank.

He drove through the residential area of Terrytown, then found a small brick house. Down the street a pack of teenagers were hanging out, but when they spotted his car, they scattered.

He climbed out then strode to the front door and knocked.

Seconds later, a clean-cut young man around eighteen opened the door. He looked like a computer geek.

"You the one who called?"

Mack nodded. "You live here alone?"

"No, my brother lives here, too."

"Where are your parents?"

The boy smirked. "Old man checked out when I was five. Mama died last year."

"You take care of your brother?"

He squared his shoulders. "I'm of age," he said as if he expected Mack to argue.

Mack shifted. The kid's life was none of his business. But he couldn't help but worry about him.

Einstein led him through a small den and kitchen. Shoes and clothes were scattered everywhere. A pizza box sat on the coffee table, soda cans beside it.

But a state-of-the-art computer system dominated the third bedroom.

Einstein obviously had a lucrative side business going.

But he'd promised the kid there wouldn't be retribution, and he'd keep his word.

Besides, what he himself was doing wasn't exactly legal.

Einstein folded his arms. "What do you want, man?"

"You know discretion works both ways," Mack said. "If I see anything on Twitter or Facebook, your side business is toast."

"No worries. Only idiots leave paper trails."

Mack chuckled. "Smart kid."

Einstein glanced at the clock, and Mack realized he'd wasted enough time chatting.

"You heard Lee Barnaby, the chief of police, was arrested?"

Einstein nodded, his eyes lighting with interest.

"I think he set me up. I need you to hack into some files for me."

"What are you looking for?"

"Anything suspicious, especially regarding the man's financials. I think he might be skimming money from the city's rebuilding fund."

"Man, that sucks." Einstein dropped into his chair.

Mack gave him Landry's name, and within seconds, Einstein retrieved his personal information, including his bank statements, social security number and all of his financial records.

"Where did you learn to do that?" Mack asked.

"Comes natural." He grinned. "What else?"

"See what you can find on Mayor Barrow."

Einstein frowned. "You think the mayor's dirty?"

"I don't know."

Einstein started tapping keys again and hacked into the mayor's personal files and business accounts.

When he finished copying the files for Mack, Mack handed Einstein a wad of cash.

Then he took the printouts and drove back to the bayou. Lily's and Winston's faces flashed in his mind as he parked at his house, and he wondered what they were doing.

Dammit, he wanted to be with them.

But first he had to prove himself to his son. When he saw him again, he didn't want anything standing between them.

LILY SPENT THE NIGHT working on the upcoming fundraiser. So far, she had persuaded three celebrities to agree to perform and several local restaurants had committed to donating food and desserts.

But the earlier confrontation involving her father and Mack and Winston haunted her.

Memories of being with Mack reminded her that their relationship was worth fighting for. He'd heated her blood the moment she'd laid eyes on him. He was so different from the men she'd dated before, so fierce and strong.

So protective.

And dangerous.

That danger had drawn her to him in a way the polite demeanor of the executives and lawyers her father had pushed on her had never done.

Her phone buzzed, and she snatched it up.

"Hello."

"Lily, this is Tate."

Speaking of lawyers and men her father wanted her to date… Her father thought his lawyer was the perfect match for Lily. He'd graduated from Harvard Law, and his salary could offer her and Winston the lifestyle her father wanted her to have.

She didn't care about that lifestyle. She wanted Winston raised with morals and solid values.

She wanted him to be the kind of man Mack was.

"What can I do for you, Tate?"

"I wondered if you needed an escort for the upcoming fund-raiser."

Lily winced. Half of the women in New Orleans would love to be Tate's date—or his wife.

But she didn't want to lead him on. "You know you're invited, but I'm afraid I'll be too busy to entertain an escort." She paused. "Besides, Tate, I'm still married."

"It's been over seven years, Lily. I told you we can have Mack declared dead."

The idea sent a shiver through her. "That's not possible, Tate. Mack is still alive."

Tate's labored sigh echoed over the line. "He's back?"

"Yes. It's a long story." And one she didn't intend to share with him. "But apparently Mack had no idea Winston and I had survived."

"They met?" Tate asked.

"Yes." Lily massaged her temple. She wished it had gone better.

"Still, Lily, it's been years. You can file for a divorce. After all, he went missing because he's a criminal."

"He wasn't convicted, Tate. In fact, he claims that Lee Barnaby arrested him on false charges."

"Come on, Lily. You aren't going to fall for his lame excuses."

Lily gritted her teeth. "Was there another reason you called?"

A sigh. "No, I just thought you and I... Face it, Lily. That cop can't give you what I can."

Lily ran a hand through her hair. No, he couldn't. Tate could give her money and fine etchings and a place in society.

Mack could give her passion, danger, excitement and...the best sex she'd ever had in her life.

"I'm worried about you and Winston," Tate continued. "If Mack loved you so much, what has he been doing all these years?

Why didn't he look for you and come back to face the charges? That's what any honest, decent man would have done."

Lily didn't intend to argue with him, especially concerning Mack. Mack was Winston's father.

And she respected that.

Looking back, she'd too easily accepted the accusations against Mack.

Now she knew Barnaby was a liar, she felt like a fool for not defending Mack.

"I appreciate your concern," Lily said, "but I can take care of myself, Tate. Now, I have another call."

She didn't give him time to respond. She hung up, her palms sweating.

First her father wanted to run her life, and now Tate?

The two of them were barely friends, more like passing business acquaintances. He handled her father's affairs, not hers.

Mack's rugged face materialized in her mind. Even if Mack wasn't in the picture now, Tate could never satisfy her the way Mack had.

She wrung her hands together, frustrated at her selfish thoughts.

Her son had to come first.

She climbed the stairs to the second floor, then peeked inside his room.

But the bed was empty.

"Winston?

Her heart raced as she flipped on the light. She searched the bed, the closet, the bathroom, then shouted his name. "Winston, where are you?"

No answer.

She ran down the steps and looked in the kitchen, then the TV room and the backyard.

But Winston was nowhere to be found.

Chapter Six

Panic immobilized Lily. Had someone abducted Winston?

Or… Winston had been so upset; what if he'd run away?

She raced to the phone and called Mack, worry clawing at her. It was late. The streets of New Orleans weren't safe. There were more murders in the city every night—

"Lily?"

"Mack, it's Winston. He's gone."

"What do you mean, *gone?*"

"He's not anywhere in the house or yard. I…thought he might have come to see you."

Mack hissed. "He doesn't know where I live. Hell, Lily, he doesn't even have my phone number."

Tears blurred Lily's eyes. "Then where is he?"

A tense pause, then she heard Mack moving around. "Does he have friends? Someone he might go to?"

"A baseball friend but he lives across town, so he wouldn't go there," Lily said.

"How about your father's house?"

"I don't think so. He heard what you said about Dad lying. He's mad at all of us."

"Call him anyway," Mack said. "I'll start combing the streets."

Lily hung up, her hand trembling as she dialed her father. If anything happened to her son, she would never forgive herself.

Horror stories about children being kidnapped, of murders, abuse and child trafficking, haunted her.

The phone rang four, then five times then rolled to voice mail. Frantic, she left a message then tried her father's cell phone, but he didn't answer that either, so she left a message on that phone as well, then ran outside. She checked the backyard, calling Winston's name repeatedly.

"Winston, if you're out here, please answer me."

But only the sound of the wind whistling echoed in the silence.

"Winston!" she shouted again. "Honey, where are you?"

She ran to the front of her house and looked up and down Saint Charles Street. Across the street lay Audubon Park. Winston loved to watch the people walking their dogs.

What if he'd gone into the park? What if he got hurt or someone kidnapped him and she never saw him again?

MACK WIPED SWEAT from his brow as he jumped into his SUV and raced toward Lily's. Surely Winston was near the house. He was mad, upset, just wanted to go somewhere and think.

He hoped to hell that was what had happened.

With Barnaby locked up and Mack asking questions, the others involved in the corruption were probably worried.

Worried enough to kidnap his son to force him to stop nosing around?

His nerves on edge, he sped around a car, the dark bayou reminding him of the evil he'd seen as a detective.

Of the people who wanted him out of the way.

God…he didn't want that evil to touch his little boy.

By the time he made the turn onto Saint Charles Street, his heart was hammering.

He slowed, searching the alleys, pausing at a stop sign to check both sides of the street. Something moved to the right, and his breath stalled as he narrowed his eyes. But a second later, a dog ran from behind a garbage can, and Mack moved on.

By the time he reached Lily's, fear consumed him. He parked on the street, jumped out and jogged up her front steps. Lily met him at the door, her face streaked with tears.

"Mack, oh God, Mack, I'm so scared."

He gripped her arms. "Shh, we'll find him," he said, praying he was right. "Any word from your father?"

"He didn't answer. But he would have called if Winston had shown up. He knows I'd be worried sick."

"Lily, look at me," Mack said, his voice firm in spite of his own terror. "Let's stay calm. You said he was angry. If he did run away, where would he go?"

She gulped back a sob. "To the park maybe. He loves it there."

Mack nodded. "Okay, I'll check the park. You stay here in case he comes back or your father calls."

"Did you call the police?" Lily asked.

Mack gritted his teeth. He didn't want to tell her that he didn't trust them. Not after the way they'd railroaded him eight years ago. "Not yet. We will if I don't find him in a few minutes"

She nodded. "Winston likes the walking trail. But he also likes the zoo."

The zoo would be closed at night, but Winston might have slipped inside. There were also more dangers waiting there. Wild animals, vagrants who slept on the benches. Drug dealers looking for a quiet place to score.

Mack jogged across the street, then ran into the park. He scanned the fountain area and walking trail. The lake drew his eye and sent another sliver of fear through him.

Dammit. He didn't even know if his son could swim.

Heart pounding, he called Winston's name then used his flashlight to illuminate the path and water.

He was halfway around the trail, near the entrance to the zoo, when his cell phone buzzed. It was Lily's number, so he snatched it up.

"Mack, Winston's at the police station."

"How did he get there?"

"Apparently, a cabdriver picked him up walking. Winston said he needed to talk to the police, and the driver didn't want to leave him on the streets so he drove him to the station. I'm going to go get him now."

"Wait," Mack said. "This is both of our mess. Winston needs to see us together."

Mack didn't give her time to argue. He jogged the rest of the way around the trail then cut across the street to Lily's. She was waiting, but the moment she saw his shattered back window, she halted.

"Mack, my God, what happened?"

Mack grimaced. In his haste to get there, he'd forgotten about the shooting. "Someone took a shot at me earlier."

Lily's eyes widened. "Someone tried to kill you?"

Mack shrugged. "Don't worry about it. I'm fine."

She rubbed her arms, her look panicked. "We're not taking your car. Not to pick up Winston."

Dear God, she was right. Being around him might endanger Winston.

"All right, let's take your car. But I'm driving."

She handed him the keys, but tension riddled the air as they sped toward the station.

Showing his face at the police station where he'd been locked up might not be a good idea.

But he was going to do it anyway.

He had to make sure his son was okay.

LILY TWISTED HER HANDS in a knot as Mack drove. Part of her wanted to punish Winston for scaring her to death.

The other part couldn't wait to hug him.

As soon as Mack parked, she jumped out of the car. Mack led the way, and they hurried into the station. They stopped at the security desk, and Lily explained about the phone call.

"Your son is in the acting chief's office right now."

Lily slanted Mack a nervous look, but his expression was closed. The receptionist led them through the doors to the bull pen, the buzz of phones and voices humming through the room. Then she knocked on the door and a minute later, gestured for them to enter the room.

Lily took one look at Winston, raced to him and pulled him into a hug. "Oh, honey, you scared me to death." She tried to stop the tears, but they overflowed anyway. "Are you all right?"

"Yes, Mom." Winston squared his little shoulders as he pulled away.

Mack hung back, his heart in his eyes, though, as he looked at his son. "You scared us both. We've been searching the streets for you."

The tall black man behind the desk cleared his throat and introduced himself as ACOP Samuel Greer. "Hold on. You need to hear what your son has to say."

Winston frowned, his dark eyes somber. "You said you used to be a policeman here, that the police framed you. I came here to find out the truth."

Mack's eyes hardened. "We'll discuss this at home, Winston."

"But I want to know," Winston said. "Are you going back to jail?"

Mack clenched his hands at his sides, but the man behind the desk spoke up. "I explained to your son that I'm new to this office. I came from Slidell. But I looked and there are no records here of your arrest."

The breath eased from Mack's chest.

Greer gestured toward Lily. "Will you take your son outside for a minute, please? I'd like to speak to Mr. Rivet alone."

Lily nodded, her stomach churning. Had he only been placating Winston? Was he going to send Mack back to prison?

MACK BRACED HIMSELF for whatever Greer planned to throw at him. If it was more charges, he'd call Remy. With Barnaby's exposed corruption, maybe he had a fighting chance at clearing himself.

"Close the door, Rivet."

Lily and Winston left, and he turned to Greer, who looked more like a football player than a police chief. But something about his eyes hinted that he was a man Mack could trust.

Still, he'd thought that before and been wrong.

"They brought me into the department when Barnaby was arrested," Greer said. "You have anything to do with that arrest?"

Mack forced himself to remain calm. "Not directly, sir. But I'm not surprised."

Greer made a low sound in his throat. "Tell me what happened eight years ago. Your side."

He wanted to know his side?

Mack took a deep breath. "Remy Comeaux and I were both detectives for the NOPD back then," Mack said. "An FBI agent named Ray Storm was investigating police corruption and corruption in the city. Remy and I worked with him on the task force to expose the corruption and the parties involved."

Greer's massive head nodded. "And—"

"The night Special Agent Storm was about to reveal the evidence he thought would bring down those involved, Lee Barnaby had me and Comeaux arrested. Katrina hit, the jails flooded…" He made a motion with his hand. "You know the rest. Files were lost. Ray Storm was pulled from the case. And I laid low, hoping to find a way to clear myself."

Greer's coal-black eyes pinned Mack to the chair.

"I was brought in here to clean up this city, and that's what I intend to do, Rivet. If you're telling the truth, I'll do everything I can to help you." He leaned forward. "But if you're one of the rotten ones, I'll see that you go to prison."

Mack gave a clipped nod. "Fair enough, sir. I will prove that I'm on the right side of the law. I always have been, always will be."

Greer hooked his thumb toward the door. "I hope for that kid's sake that you are."

Mack nodded again, then shook the man's hand and left the room. When he spotted Lily, she looked shaken.

"Let's go home," he said, then realized he didn't live with them. That irked him, but tonight wasn't the time to push, not when Lily looked ragged and his little boy exhausted.

He escorted them back to Lily's then walked with them inside. When they entered, Winston started to climb the steps, but Mack asked him to stay for a minute.

He looked wary, as if he was expecting some punishment to be doled out. "Let's sit down and talk," Mack said.

They all filed into her den, a cozy room with comfortable chairs and a denim couch. Winston collapsed onto it, but he chewed his lip as if he was nervous.

"Winston, we're glad you're safe," Mack said. "But you scared your mother and me both tonight."

Winston started to speak, but Mack held up his hand. "I know I haven't been around the last few years, but that's not because

I didn't want to be. Unfortunately, we all have to accept that Katrina tore us apart."

Winston looked at Lily and she conceded with a nod.

"But I am here now and I'm going to be part of your life. So don't ever run off on your own like that, especially at night."

Winston started to object but Mack remained firm. "I mean it. Your mom was frantic, and she had a right to be. It's dangerous—"

"I'm not a baby anymore," Winston said.

"No, but you're also not an adult. And I worked in this town long enough to know what can happen to a kid, to a grown-up even, when they're alone at night."

"I got it," Winston said, an edge to his voice.

Mack liked his spunk, but he also had to rein the boy in. "Do you understand?"

Winston nodded.

Mack squatted down in front of his son. "If there's anything you want to know, just come to your mother or me." He tilted Winston's chin toward him. "I promise I will tell you the truth."

Winston stared into his eyes for a minute, questions lingering. "You didn't do what they said?"

Mack shook his head. "No, son, and I'll prove it. Just give me a chance. I want to be a father to you. I want to take you fishing and out to my place in the bayou and you can ride in my pirogue."

Winston perked up. "I can steer the boat?"

Mack chuckled. "Yes, you can."

Then he ruffled Winston's hair and told him good-night.

When Winston disappeared up the steps, Lily followed to tuck him in. Mack paced the den, unable to make himself leave.

His family, the woman he'd loved and his son, were here.

But he lived miles away. Maybe farther in her heart.

The sound of Lily's footsteps echoed on the stairs, her face glowing in the lamplight as she returned.

She looked so damn beautiful that she took his breath away.

"Thank you for tonight, Mack," she said softly. "I was scared out of my mind."

"Me, too," he said.

She shivered, and he pulled her into his arms. "He's going to be okay," he whispered. "You've done a good job with him, Lily."

Lily's expression mirrored his own emotions. "You should have been there with him when he was born...when he learned to walk..."

He cupped her face in his. "I know, and I wish I had been. But I'm here now."

Unshed tears glistened on her eyelashes, then a breath escaped her, a sigh of need following.

That sigh was all he needed.

He closed his mouth over hers.

Chapter Seven

Lily parted her lips for Mack. His strong arms encircled her, drawing her against his chest. Heat flared inside her as he ran his hands over her hips.

He groaned, the sound a heady aphrodisiac to a woman who hadn't had a lover in eight years.

Because no one had measured up to Mack.

His tongue made a foray into her mouth, teasing her as one hand rose to slide over her breast. Her nipple instantly hardened, hunger and need mounting.

Then he started to unbutton her blouse, and she realized where they were, that Winston could come down the steps at any minute.

"Mack," she whispered against his ear. "Winston—"

He pulled back enough to look into her face. "You want me to stop?"

The emotions and desire in his eyes made her blood sizzle. She had loved him and lost him, and missed him and wanted him back so badly. She couldn't stop now.

"No, my room."

"Upstairs?"

She shook her head. "To the left."

The lecherous, bad-boy grin that had always stolen her soul flared, and he swung her into his arms and carried her into the room. When he threw her onto the bed, he tore at her clothes. Heat rippled between them, the passion so intense her skin tingled as if it was on fire.

He stripped her, then paused to look his fill. Lily shivered at his blatant perusal, smiling as he removed his shirt.

She'd always loved his body, the way his muscles rippled across his chest, the way his arms bulged, the way the planes in his face strained when he held back from rushing their love-making.

He had that look now.

She thought she'd never forget his body, but it was even more masculine than she remembered. Not an ounce of fat, just sinewy muscle and bold, taut lines.

And his sex, it seemed bigger, thicker, longer…

She wanted it inside her, filling her, reminding her they'd been married, that he had loved her and she loved him.

Another sinful look crossed his face, then he lowered himself beside her. Her breath caught as he slowly trailed his fingers over her skin, teasing her. Shivers ran up her spine, then he licked his way along all the tender places he'd touched, and Lily's body trembled.

But two could play that game, and she tortured him the same way.

He hissed between his teeth as she straddled him, her breasts swaying, heavy and achy, her nipples jutting toward him in need.

He teased them with his fingers, his gaze latching onto hers.

"Mack," she whispered, hurting for him.

His eyes danced with mischief, then he took one nipple between his teeth and suckled her while he explored her inner thighs with his fingers. Lily threaded her hands into his hair and pulled him to her, rocking herself on his hand.

Seconds later, he flipped her over and pushed his sex between her thighs.

"I missed you so much," he murmured as he thrust inside her.

"I missed you, too." His length filled her, driving her to the brink, then he pulled out and thrust inside her again.

She moaned, nearly coming apart as he lifted her legs around his waist and pushed deeper, so deep that her orgasm rippled through her.

Mack pulled out again, then paused. "Dammit, a condom."

She didn't care about a condom or if they had another baby. All she wanted was him inside her now.

She slid her fingers around his length, and he jerked toward her, the heat between them so intense that he plunged into her, filling her to the core.

She groaned his name, then looked into his eyes as his release rippled through him, his groan of pleasure echoing in the air.

MACK MADE LOVE TO LILY over and over through the night. He couldn't get enough.

But finally in the wee hours of the morning, Lily fell asleep. For a long while, he simply watched her. She was so beautiful and strong and was such a good mother to their son.

He wanted to be with her and with Winston as he should have been all along.

But first he had to prove that he was worthy of them.

Reality interceded, and he eased from bed, dressed, then went outside to his car. He retrieved the files Einstein had hacked into for him, brought them into the house and brewed a pot of coffee.

He spent the next few hours studying each fundraiser and meeting Landry had had in the past few years. Then he turned to Landry's financials. His father-in-law kept a hefty checking and savings account, and had set up one primary account for the rebuilding fund.

Then he noticed several other businesses Landry had established. Landry was an entrepreneur, but Mack was still curious, so he did a Google search of the first one and found a website but no product. He called the phone number but a recording clicked on saying the number was no longer in service.

Mack went down the list, studying the bank accounts for each corporation, then spent the next couple of hours trying to verify the businesses. But he couldn't find any evidence that the companies were legitimate. He found a Swiss bank account in the name of one of the dummy corporations. A Swiss account attached to Landry's name.

Damn. His father-in-law was in big trouble.

He studied the mayor's accounts next and found discrepancies there, as well.

He went back eight years and analyzed their accounts and realized several of the companies had been set up pre-Katrina, meaning Landry and the mayor had been laundering money for years.

When the mayor established the rebuilding fund, they'd immediately started skimming money from it.

A little more digging, and anger set in. A notation next to his name indicated that Landry had paid an anonymous source fifty thousand dollars a week before the flood hit.

Proof that Landry had paid someone to frame him.

Mack had to go to the police.

But if he had Landry arrested, he would hurt Lily and his son.

Still, it was time for the truth to come out.

He picked up the phone to make the call.

He was going to fight for the woman he loved and his son.

He just hoped Lily didn't hate him when she found out he'd turned her father in.

LILY WOKE TO AN EMPTY BED. She inhaled Mack's scent on the sheets and missed him already. Sun glimmered through the lacy sheers of her room, and the scent of coffee and bacon filled the air.

She pulled on a robe, splashed cold water on her face and ran a brush through her hair. It was so tangled she finally pulled it back in a ponytail, the memory of making love to Mack so fresh that she wanted him again.

Maybe Winston was still asleep and she and Mack could crawl back into bed.

She hurried into the kitchen but found Winston at the table, making a bacon-and-egg sandwich just like Mack had on his plate.

They looked so much alike that her heart squeezed. They even had the same scowl as they bit into the breakfast sandwich.

Mack looked up at her, the twinkle in his eyes making her body tingle with need again. But a second later, worry darkened his expression.

"Look, Mom, Dad cooked breakfast."

Dad. The fact that Winston used that endearment told her how much he wanted a father.

"I see." Lily smiled. It was such a normal, everyday ritual to share a morning meal. But it was something else Mack and Winston had missed. All the mornings and days and nights together.

She poured herself a cup of coffee, then noticed a file on the table. But Mack grabbed it and shoved it down into an accordion file folder beside him.

She frowned, then the phone jangled, and she saw her father's name, so she answered. "Dad, I'm sorry I called so late—"

"What's this about Winston? Is he all right?"

"Yes, Dad. It's a long story, but he's fine."

"Good, but I have a problem, Lily. Call my lawyer immediately."

Lily tensed at his terse tone. "What's going on?"

"The police are here with an arrest warrant and warrants to search my house and computer."

Lily's heart stuttered. "What? What are they accusing you of?"

"Money laundering and framing your husband."

Lily gasped, then turned toward Mack. He couldn't have had anything do with it, could he?

Regret flickered in his eyes for a second before his expression shut down. Her stomach knotted.

"Get Tate now," her father said. "And, Lily, if you see Rivet, don't say anything to him. And for God's sake, don't let him near your computer."

A chill slithered up Lily's spine. She didn't have anything to hide, so why was her father worried?

Then anger mushroomed inside her. Had Mack already looked at her computer?

Was that the reason he'd come inside last night and slept with her?

Chapter Eight

Lily's heart sank as she stared at Mack.

She'd never imagined he'd use her to find something bad against her father, that he hated him that much.

She wanted to lash out, but after Winston's escapade the night before, she had to watch what she said in front of him.

So she stepped into the hallway to call Tate. Mack was watching her, but she turned away from him as she made the call. Then she phoned Winston's friend's mother asking for him to stay with them.

When she returned to the kitchen, Winston was finishing his breakfast. "Honey, get dressed. I'm going to drop you off at Drew's house."

Winston looked confused. "Why can't I just hang out with Dad?"

Mack opened his mouth to speak, but she shot him a warning look. "He has work to do. You can see him later."

Mack patted Winston's back. "Your mom's right. We'll hang out tonight or tomorrow. I promise."

Winston accepted what he said and ran up the steps. Lily grabbed the file.

"You used me last night to gain access to my computer." Hurt hardened her voice. "How could you? I…" She'd thought he wanted her back.

Mack closed his fingers around her wrist. "It wasn't like that, Lily. I've never stopped loving you—"

"You don't betray someone you love." She glanced down at the files. The printout showed her father's financial information. "What is this anyway?"

Mack sighed. "Eight years ago I was working on a task force

to blow the lid on police corruption. I think Barnaby framed me because I was getting too close."

"What does this have to do with my father?" Lily asked sharply.

Mack scraped a hand over his jaw, the sound of his beard stubble grazing his hand a reminder that they'd spent the night together. That she'd given herself to him out of trust and love, and he'd broken that trust. "There are dummy companies set up in your father's name," Mack said. "It appears that he and the mayor are laundering money."

Lily gasped. "Why would my father steal money?"

"I don't know. Greed maybe." He shrugged. "But according to this, they're skimming money that you're raising for rebuilding."

Lily shook her head in denial. "I don't believe you, Mack."

Mack's eyes went cold. "Just like last time." Bitterness laced his voice. "I should have known you'd side with him."

"It's not about choosing sides," Lily said. "I know my father. He loves this city and cares too much about helping New Orleans to do what you're suggesting."

"And you don't know me?" Mack said. "You didn't know me back then?"

Lily didn't know what to say. She should have believed in him when they'd arrested him. "I'm sorry, Mack. I know I hurt you. Is that why you're doing this? To get back at me for not standing up for you?"

"No," Mack snapped. "I'm trying to clear my name so my son will look up to me."

He snatched his jacket then headed to the door. Lily watched him go, her heart breaking.

FOR THE FIRST TIME in a long time, Mack wanted to be wrong about Landry. He hated hurting Lily but couldn't ignore the evidence.

He drove home and showered, then went to the precinct. When he arrived, he found Lily pacing inside. Apparently her father and his lawyer were being interrogated.

"Lily—"

She gave him a sizzling look. "Don't bother, Mack."

"You don't understand—"

"I understand perfectly," Lily said, cutting him off. "Just one question. Do you think your son would be proud of what you did today?"

Mack felt as if he'd been punched in the gut.

Before he could respond, the door opened and Landry walked out with a man who had to be his attorney. His manicure alone indicated he'd never done a hard day's work in his life.

Landry scowled at Mack. "I figured you were behind this."

The lawyer glared at Mack. "So you're Mack Rivet?"

Mack nodded. "I haven't had the pleasure."

"Tate Manning," the young man said. "You made a big mistake coming after Mr. Landry."

"I didn't come after him," Mack said. "I'm just searching for the truth."

Lily hugged her father. "I'm so sorry, Dad."

"Don't worry, honey. I'll take care of this." He released her and turned to Mack. "How did you get into my files? Did you use my daughter?"

Mack shook his head. "No. Lily has nothing to do with this."

"She has everything to do with it," Landry said. "For all I know you fabricated evidence to create doubt in her mind so she'd turn to you."

"I wouldn't do that," Mack said. "Barnaby's arrest proves there's corruption in the city. Hell, half of New Orleans's officials may be involved."

Landry's eyes narrowed. "Be careful where you make accusations, Rivet."

Manning moved closer to Lily, a protective gleam in his eyes, and Mack realized that his involvement was personal. At least Manning wanted it to be.

Dammit, had he and Lily been seeing each other?

"I suggest you stay away from my client and his daughter," Manning said. "And just so you know, these charges will be dropped before you can blink."

Lily took her father's arm, and Manning inched up beside her as they left.

Hell, Manning might get the charges dropped, especially if Landry or the mayor owned someone in the department or a judge.

Then he'd be back to square one. Worse, he would have lost Lily's trust.

What good would it do him to get his name back if he lost her and Winston?

LILY TRIED TO MOVE AWAY from Tate's constant hovering as they walked outside.

"Everything's going to be fine," Manning assured her and her father. "Before this is over, Rivet will be brought up on charges."

"What charges?" Lily asked. It wasn't as if he'd broken into her place to access her computer.

"I don't know yet, but however he obtained that information, it was illegal."

Lily's father exchanged a worried look with her. "Let's just clear me, then we'll worry about what to do about him."

"How about lunch?" Manning said. "I'll treat you both."

"Sure, we can discuss strategy," her father said.

Lily begged off. She didn't want to encourage Tate. "I have to pick up Winston." She kissed her dad's cheek. "I'll talk to you later."

He squeezed her arm, and she hurried away before Tate could mention the fundraiser, again.

She was perspiring by the time she reached her car.

What was she going to tell Winston?

Hopefully nothing about her father's legal problems. Maybe he would have them solved soon and there would be no need.

She had a few hours until she picked Winston up, so she met with the restaurant owners to finalize the menu.

It was dark by the time she reached Winston's friend's house. When Winston climbed into the car, he babbled excitedly about playing ball and video games at his friend's house.

"I'm glad you had fun," she said. "Next time, we'll have Drew over to our house."

She called in a pizza order, then stopped to pick it up a few minutes later. When they arrived at the house, he took the box as she unlocked the door.

She reached for the light but the scent of a man's aftershave assaulted her. Not her father's or Mack's. Then the floor squeaked.

She tensed and clutched Winston's arm.

Someone was inside.

Before she could tell her son to run, the intruder shoved a gun to her temple.

MACK'S PHONE WAS RINGING by the time he made it back to the bayou so he snatched it up.

"Hello."

"If you want to see your wife and son again, you'd better listen."

Mack's heart stopped. "Who is this? Let me speak to Lily."

"Call the cops and they're dead."

"What do you want?"

"Make the charges against Landry go away, then stop asking questions."

Sweat trickled down his back. "Done. But only if you let me talk to my family so I know they're safe."

A noise sounded then Lily's voice. "Mack."

"Are you and Winston all right?"

"Yes," she whispered. "But Winston misses that alligator we bought him at Mardi Gras."

Mack frowned.

She must be trying to send him a message.

"I'll take care of it."

"Mack—"

Another noise, then Lily's voice protesting, and a heartbeat later, the man's voice returned. "I'll be in touch."

Mack cursed as the phone clicked into silence.

Chapter Nine

Lily pulled her son to her, tensing as the man pointed the gun at her. "Please don't hurt us."

"Cooperate and I won't."

She nodded, playing along until she could figure out a way for them to escape. So far, he'd made her drive them to the city, then forced them to climb some stairs in a deserted building.

He shoved them into a small room and locked the door.

Winston looked up at her with terrified eyes. "Mom?"

"It's going to be okay," she said, although fear had seized her the moment the man had pressed the gun to her temple.

"Don't worry. Dad will save us."

Lily gave him a hug. Winston had such confidence, as if he believed Mack could save the world. Maybe they'd connected more than she'd realized.

Still, she scanned the room, looking for something to use as a weapon.

The room was devoid of furniture, though, and she saw nothing to use to defend them.

The French Quarter stretched below them, the sounds of tourists, traffic and music loud enough to drown out a scream if she yelled for help.

She tried to open the window, but it wouldn't budge. In fact, it looked as if it had been painted shut. She considered breaking the window, but she couldn't risk that the man holding them might hear.

Bright lights from the voodoo store below twirled colors across the night sky.

She only hoped Mack figured out the reason she'd told him to get the stuffed alligator.

It might be the only way he would find them.

She didn't trust their kidnapper to keep his word. For all she knew, once Mack did what he'd requested, the man would kill her and Winston.

MACK STRUGGLED TO CALM HIMSELF as he hurried to his SUV. Lily had told him about the alligator for a reason. He just wished to hell he knew what it was.

Palms sweating, he flew onto the freeway toward New Orleans, weaving through traffic and speeding around slower vehicles.

When he reached Lily's, he went straight to Winston's room. He paused in the doorway, scanning the bed and shelves for a stuffed alligator.

On the bed, he spotted a bear and stuffed dog, but no reptile. Then he noticed a soccer-ball-shaped toy chest in the corner.

He lifted the lid and dug inside, plowing through toy cars and trucks, several packs of baseball cards, a football and a magic set. Relief filled him when he spotted a green tail. He pulled it out and examined the toy, but couldn't find a tag or anything to indicate where Lily and Winston might be.

Frustrated, he contemplated what to do. He hadn't been with Lily at Mardi Gras, but he'd seen the picture—her father had been there. As much as he hated to see the man, he needed his help.

He jogged down the steps, then jumped into his car and drove to Landry's. Minutes later, he screeched into Landry's drive, then rushed to the door and pounded on it, ringing the doorbell and beating his fist against it at the same time.

The lights were off, but he pounded again, and suddenly lights flickered on. Shuffling sounded inside, then the door opened. Landry was wearing a bathrobe, his hair rumpled.

"What in the hell are you doing here?"

Mack pushed his way past Landry. "We have to talk."

"It's midnight," Landry said. "You have a lot of nerve—"

"Someone kidnapped Lily and Winston," Mack shouted.

Landry staggered back, one hand flying to his chest. "You're lying."

"I wish I was. But a man called me a few minutes ago. He

said he has Lily and Winston and that he'll only release them if I get the charges against you dropped and stop asking questions."

Landry paled. "God...I can't believe this."

Mack shook him. "Do you know who's holding them?"

"Of course not," Landry said. "How can you ask me such a horrible thing?"

Mack lifted the stuffed alligator.

"I talked to Lily for a second, and she mentioned this alligator. It must have some significance."

"I bought it for Winston in the Quarter."

"Where?" Mack asked.

Landry looked panicked for a moment. "I don't remember exactly. They were selling them on the street."

"Dammit, think," Mack said. "Was there a restaurant nearby? Another store?"

Landry rubbed his forehead. "A voodoo shop. Winston liked the colors swirling in the window." He snapped his fingers. "It was down from the market."

"He must be holding them somewhere near there. Maybe an abandoned storefront."

"I can get copies of the downtown area and the abandoned properties," Landry suggested.

Mack nodded. "I'll call the acting chief of police and tell them that I fabricated the financial files they have."

Landry's eyes widened. "Did you fabricate them?"

"No," Mack said firmly. "But I'll do anything to save Lily and Winston."

Landry stared at him for a long moment. "So will I, Rivet. And whether you believe it or not, I did not steal money from the city's rebuilding fund. I may be wealthy now, but I didn't grow up with money. I earned every penny I have."

Mack swallowed hard. As much as he'd battled with the man, he believed him. "But there were dummy corporations set up that the money went into," Mack said. "Who else had access to your records?"

Landry's jaw tightened. "My attorney Tate also has an accounting degree, so he handles everything for me." He paused. "But he would never hurt Lily. He likes her."

"He probably likes his freedom better. And if he's taking money from your funds, he's probably afraid the police will figure it out."

"So he's desperate." Landry headed into his office. "I'll call him right now."

Mack followed him, grateful they were finally working on the same side. "Wait," Mack said. "If we tip him off, he might tell the thug holding Lily and Winston and he'll hurt them."

Landry exhaled a shaky breath. "Then what should we do?"

"Set up a meeting with Manning and the mayor in the morning. Tell them it's urgent." He'd convince Landry to wear a wire so they could get the dirt on both of them.

If he caught Manning red-handed, he'd have to tell him where Lily and Winston were.

"Now, show me those city plans. I'm going after them tonight."

LILY PACED FOR A WHILE, but her agitation was only making Winston more frightened, so she sat down and pulled him beside her. She rolled up her jacket and gave it to him as a pillow.

"Tell me about Dad," Winston said as he settled down.

Lily rubbed his shoulders. "Your father was a good policeman. In fact, he made detective sooner than most."

"How did you meet him?"

God, it seemed like a lifetime ago. She'd been so young. "I was in college at Tulane," she said. "There were several car break-ins on campus, then a couple of girls were assaulted. One of the victims lived on my hallway in the dorm. Campus security called in the NOPD and your father showed up."

The moment she'd seen him, all tall, muscular and rugged, she'd fallen for him. "He just took charge," Lily said. "He was calm, and he reassured the girl the police would find her attacker—and he did the very next week."

Winston hugged her. "He'll find us, too, Mom. I know he will."

Lily stroked a strand of hair from his forehead. But the stubborn lock fell back, just as Mack's used to do. "I know, honey. So try to sleep. Maybe in the morning we can go home."

Winston yawned, then rolled to his side.

She only hoped he was right that Mack would find them.

A second later Winston fell asleep, and she went to the window. Outside, partiers strolled by as if they didn't have a care in the world. She wanted to beat on the glass and scream for help, but doing that would only bring their kidnapper running.

She wanted to fight him, but he was a hundred pounds heavier than her and had a loaded weapon.

She couldn't take a chance on him hurting her son.

MACK STUDIED THE LAYOUT of the buildings in the Quarter while Landry drew a red circle around the area where he'd purchased the alligator.

"There," Landry said as he pointed to the top floor above two storefronts. "That space is empty. It's been for sale for months."

"Manning would know about it?"

Landry nodded.

Mack checked his weapon and headed toward the door.

"Rivet?"

Mack's pulse pounded as he paused. "Yes?"

"Bring my daughter and grandson home safely."

Mack looked him square in the eye. "I'll save them or die trying."

Landry's face twisted with emotions, but Mack didn't have time to deal with it. He jogged to his car, then drove to the Quarter. The town was lit up, the partiers in full swing. He parked, then tugged on a baseball hat as he walked through the streets toward the market.

As he approached the storefront, he kept his head low in case Lily's kidnapper was watching, then slipped into the alley.

A window faced the back. A small patio was attached with wrought-iron rails.

Then he saw the face in the window and his heart hammered. Lily.

She saw him at the same time he spotted her, then waved her

hands frantically. He threw up a hand to let her know he saw her, then jumped up to reach the bottom rung of the fire escape.

Dammit, he hated heights, but he'd have to manage.

One by one he climbed the steps, then he plastered himself against the narrow ledge along the building, forcing himself not to look at the ground as he inched toward the wrought-iron rail surrounding the patio. He released a pent-up breath when he reached it, then climbed over the rail.

Lily looked scared but brave as she pressed her hand against the windowpane.

He was relieved to see Winston asleep on the floor. He gestured to Lily to open the window, but she mouthed that it was painted shut.

Dammit.

It was so old it looked as if the wood was rotting around the glass, so he removed his knife and tried to slide it between the edges of the glass and wood, hoping to pry it open.

But that didn't work, either.

Finally he motioned for her to move back from the window. She did, huddled beside Winston. Mack removed a handkerchief from his pocket, wrapped it around his hand and gently hit the glass. Fragments shattered, then he repeated the motion. Winston jerked awake and watched wide-eyed.

When he'd broken all the glass, Mack crawled inside, but just as his feet hit the floor, the door opened and a big man carrying a gun rushed inside.

He took one look at Mack and fired the .38.

LILY SCREAMED AND COVERED Winston. Mack ducked to avoid the shot. The kidnapper lunged toward her with his gun pointed.

"Drop it or they both get it," the man barked.

Mack held up his hands in surrender, then laid his gun on the floor. The man inched close enough to kick it away.

Winston glared at the man, while Lily held him tight.

"What are you going to do? Kill us all?" Mack asked.

"If I have to."

"You're going to jail!" Winston shouted. "My dad will see to it you rot in prison."

The man jerked his head sideways for a split second, and Mack took advantage of the moment.

He knocked him backward. The man's gun flew across the room, then he and Mack rolled on the floor, trading blows.

Mack was big, but this guy was monstrous.

The jerk slammed his fist into Mack's nose and blood spurted, but Mack delivered a karate chop to the kidnapper's neck that made the bastard bellow in pain.

Then Mack flipped him to his back, punched him in the face and pinned him with his legs. One grunt and the man bucked Mack off him and sent him slamming into the wall.

He crawled for the gun as Mack caught his breath. Lily released Winston and kicked the weapon toward Mack. He snatched it and aimed it at the man.

"Make one move and I'll shoot," Mack snarled.

The man grunted but raised his hands. Mack inched slowly toward him, then snagged handcuffs from his pocket and cuffed the man's arms behind him.

"Are you two okay?" Mack asked Lily.

"Yes." Lily helped Winston stand and they inched over beside him.

"I knew you'd come, Dad," Winston said.

Lily smiled shakily. She had known he would, too.

MACK'S MOUTH SLID INTO A GRIN. His boy was going to be tough like him. And Lily was brave, too.

Mack wanted to be part of both of their lives forever.

"This isn't over," the bastard snarled.

Mack gripped his cell phone while he kept the gun trained on the man. "It will be soon. You can make it easier on yourself if you confess who hired you."

"I'm not telling you anything."

Mack shrugged. "You're going to be sitting in jail for a long time, buddy."

The man cursed, then spit blood as Mack dialed Remy's number.

Ten minutes later Remy appeared with Greer, and they took the man into custody.

Lily borrowed his phone to call her father while Mack explained things to Greer. Then he confiscated the kidnapper's phone. "I'm going to keep this in case the person who hired him calls back. If it's who I think it is, we don't want to tip him off that he lost his leverage."

Greer nodded, then agreed to meet him at Landry's the next morning. "I'll need your statements, too," he told Lily.

She rubbed Winston's shoulder. He had been tough, but he looked exhausted. "I'll come down tomorrow. Right now I want to take my son home to bed."

"I'll drive you," Mack said.

He carried Winston and they walked to the car together.

Winston fell asleep in the backseat as soon as Mack started the engine. "What's going on tomorrow?" Lily asked.

Mack explained about the setup, and anger flickered across Lily's face. "You think Tate is the one who skimmed the funds?"

Mack nodded. "I also think the gubernatorial candidate is involved."

Lily looked shocked, but the day had worn on her, too, and she didn't argue.

"This plan sounds dangerous," she said as they arrived at her house. "Mack, I don't want my father hurt."

Mack reached over and did what he'd wanted to do all night. He pulled her into a hug, his body still reeling from seeing that gun trained on her and his little boy. Lily was trembling, as well.

"I promise you that I won't let anything happen to him," he whispered.

He just hoped to hell he could keep that promise.

Chapter Ten

Lily encouraged Winston to stay at his friend's house the next morning, but he stubbornly refused. "I want to be with you and Dad," he insisted. "I'm not a kid anymore."

If anything could make a child grow up fast, she supposed it was a kidnapping.

"All right, but you're going to the batting cage with Anita while Grandpa has his meeting. I don't want you in the house."

He pouted but realized it was futile to argue. She didn't intend to have her son anywhere near the danger again.

She met Mack and Greer at eight and watched them wire her father's office. Mack had installed a camera in the office, which infuriated her and her father when he realized it. But they agreed to allow it to remain intact for the purpose of the meeting.

She and Mack and Greer waited in the den with the door closed, but thanks to technology, they had a good view via her father's computer. The atmosphere was thick with tension as Tate and the mayor joined her father.

"What's this about?" Mayor Barrow asked.

"You heard I was brought in to the police station for questioning about my financial records," her father said.

"Yes," Mayor Barrow answered. "But Manning assured me that you would be cleared."

"That's right," Tate said with a smug grin.

"Just how do you plan to do that?" her father asked. "It sounds like they have solid evidence against me."

Tate paced the room. "Don't worry, Landry. I took care of that."

"What do you mean?" her father asked.

Tate smiled again. "I made sure that Rivet clears you."

The mayor rubbed his balding head, his brows furrowed. "How so?"

"That jerk is going to tell the police that he fabricated the evidence. Rivet will wind up in jail and you'll go free."

Her father's jaw hardened. Tate had practically admitted to arranging the kidnapping to force Mack into covering up their illegal activities.

"But he didn't fabricate it, did he?" her father asked.

"That doesn't matter," Tate said. "You'll be cleared and he goes to jail. It's a win-win for all of us."

"You're sure about this?" Mayor Barrow asked. "Because if those files get examined by the wrong people, we're in trouble."

"Good God," Greer said. "You were right, Rivet. The mayor *is* stealing money from the city funds."

Mayor Barrow paced. "I can't believe you left a paper trail."

"Let me get this straight. You set this up, Tate, so you could steal from the rebuilding funds?" Her father glanced at the mayor. "And you knew about it?"

"Don't worry, Melvin," Mayor Barrow said. "We'll cut you in. There's plenty to go around."

"Shut up." Tate's nostrils flared as he grabbed her father by the collar. "What's going on, Landry?"

Her father gritted his teeth. "I trusted you. I even encouraged my daughter to go out with you, but you stole from me, and then you had Lily and Winston kidnapped as leverage."

Lily grabbed Mack's arm. "I don't like this, Mack."

"Me, either." Mack jerked his thumb toward Greer. "Let's go."

They moved toward the door, but Tate drew a gun on her father.

"Stay here, Lily," Mack ordered.

Greer pulled his weapon, and Mack did the same, then they hurried into the hallway toward Landry's office.

She held her breath, praying Tate didn't panic and open fire.

MACK HAD PROMISED LILY he wouldn't let anything happen to her father. He had to keep his promise.

Greer swung open the office door, his weapon drawn. "Put the gun down, Mr. Manning. It's over."

Panic and shock flared in Manning's eyes, but the mayor threw up his hands.

"This man has been stealing from the city," Mayor Barrow shouted. "I had nothing to do with it."

"Don't bother lying, Mayor Barrow," Greer said. "We have you all on tape."

"You can't use that in court," Manning screeched. "We have rights."

"So do the people you stole from," Mack said between clenched teeth.

Greer stepped toward Manning, but Manning swung the gun up and fired. Mack shoved Greer out of the way and fired at Manning. The bullet pierced Manning's leg, and he bellowed and dropped his gun.

Mack kicked the gun out of the way, then spun Manning around and shoved him against the wall. Greer pushed himself up from the floor and stalked toward the mayor, then handcuffed him.

A moment later Lily rushed in and threw herself at her father. "Daddy, are you okay?"

"Yes, baby." He enveloped her in his arms while Mack and Greer hauled Manning and the mayor to the squad car they'd hidden in Landry's garage.

Landry appeared a moment later. "Rivet?"

Mack glanced up and saw Lily and Winston standing behind him. Then Landry extended his hand. "I was wrong about you. Thank you for saving my daughter and grandson."

Emotions thickened Mack's throat. He'd never expected an apology from Landry. "No problem."

Then Lily threw her arms around him. "I was so mad at you, Mack, but I missed you so much. And I still love you."

His heart stuttered as he swept her into his arms. "I love you, too, Lily."

Greer cleared his throat, then gestured toward the police car. "I've got this, Rivet. Why don't you stay here with your family?"

Mack nodded, then looked at Lily with questions in his eyes. "Lily? Can you forgive me?"

She smiled and kissed him, and he had his answer.

He returned the kiss with all the love he'd held inside for eight years.

When they finally pulled apart, Winston vaulted into his arms. Mack choked back tears and hugged his family to him.

Eight years ago he'd lost them.

Now that he had them back, he'd never let them go again.

* * * * *

MALLORY KANE

BAYOU JUSTICE

CAST OF CHARACTERS

Ray Storm—The dedicated FBI agent abandoned New Orleans and Molly Hennessey when Katrina hit. Now he's back, to bring a corrupt public figure to justice. But solving his case will not only break Molly's heart and his own, it could get them both killed.

Molly Hennessey—Molly was young and in love when undercover agent Ray Storm seduced her into revealing incriminating secrets about her brother, then disappeared when Hurricane Katrina hit New Orleans. Now Ray is back, with danger and heartache in tow. Torn between loyalty to her family and telling the truth, Molly knows that no matter which side she chooses, she will be left with a broken heart.

Angelica DePuye—An addict and a confidential informant before Hurricane Katrina, Angel turned her life around and became a cop. She works for the Narcotics division of the New Orleans Police Department now and knows a lot about who's who and where they are in New Orleans.

Martin Hennessey—Eight years ago, this head of the Louisiana Disaster Avoidance Task Force (LDAT) was saved from indictment for stealing Federal grant monies earmarked to shore up New Orleans levees when Hurricane Katrina washed away the FBI's evidence against him. Eight years later, the FBI agent is back, and Martin can see his plans to be governor of Louisiana crumbling.

Joseph Flay—Ray Storm could not uncover a shred of evidence against this Louisiana Disaster Avoidance Task Force (LDAT) attorney eight years ago. Flay has not been seen since Katrina and is presumed dead. But is he?

Brian LeFay—Martin Hennessey's campaign manager and the brains behind his gubernatorial campaign. But LeFay has no past prior to Katrina. Who is he, and what does he hope to gain by putting Hennessey into the governor's mansion?

Remy Comeaux—Private detective and former NOPD narcotics detective.

Mack Rivet—Former NOPD detective involved with the FBI investigation with Remy Comeaux and Ray Storm.

To Michael, for always.

Chapter One

Ray Storm dodged a pair of college girls on bikes sporting Tulane backpacks and frowned as he looked at the hamburger joint that sat exactly where his apartment had been back on August 29, 2005, the day Hurricane Katrina hit New Orleans. The corner of Octavia and Freret streets was almost unrecognizable. Not surprising, but disconcerting.

He'd watched the coverage 24/7, like everyone who had been in New Orleans on that day. Later, he'd watched the in-depth news stories and the TV specials, and because he'd been an FBI agent, he'd read top secret memos and reports unavailable to the general public.

Now, eight years later, he stared at where he'd lived then, struck anew by the knowledge that not only had Katrina changed New Orleans and the world forever, she had changed him, as well.

Before his brain could start down the dangerous path of how different things might have been if that particular storm hadn't struck on that particular night in that particular city, a striking, vaguely familiar figure caught his eye. A tall woman with café au lait skin, dressed in slim jeans and red platform heels, emerged from between two massive Hollywood South eighteen-wheelers, dragging every male gaze away from the bustle of director chairs, booms and cameras in her wake. Ray shook his head in wonder at the woman he'd known eight years ago as a hopped-up C.I.

Another life changed by Katrina, that graceless lady.

Angelica DePuye didn't stop until her nose was less than two inches from his. She propped her fists on her slim hips. "I swear to Pete. You are alive and breathing. I thought I'd gotten a call from beyond the grave." She smiled. "You might be surprised at how often that happens these days."

Ray put his hands on her shoulders and took a step backward, eyeing her with his brows raised. "Looks like the past eight years have been good to you, Angel."

"Humph," she snorted delicately and tossed her head, sending the sleek ponytail anchored at the crown of her head swishing, then kissed his cheek. "You can call me Officer DePuye," she retorted, sliding a hand into her jeans pocket and slipping the edge of an instantly recognizable black leather case free for an instant. "But not in public. These days I'm a narc."

Her mouth was twisted in a mocking smile, but Ray saw the pride in her dark eyes. "No way," he said. "That's great."

Before Katrina, Angel had been a heroin addict and NOPD officer Mack Rivet's confidential informant. She shrugged. "After Katrina, I lost my C.I. cred, and believe it or not, it was damned hard to find H at any price." She shrugged as she tucked the badge case back into her pocket. "I had to do something."

"Something," Ray echoed, a chuckle in his voice. "Which in your case was merely to get sober and enter the police academy."

"Well, it wasn't as easy as it sounds. Buy me a cup of coffee," she said, gesturing toward the café with a toss of her ponytail, "and tell me what's brought your Yankee butt down here again."

They went into the burger joint, where, with the exception of the scowling man behind the counter, they were the oldest by at least ten years. All the customers and most of the waitstaff had the earnest, freshly washed faces of college students.

Ray gestured for two coffees, then sat back. "A lot has changed."

"First words out of everybody's mouth when they come back," Angel commented.

The waitress set the thick white cups in front of them and managed to mumble something and pop her gum at the same time.

"Might be a cliché, but it's true," he said, shaking his head at the girl, figuring there was a 90 percent chance she'd asked if they needed anything else. Once she'd moved on to the next table, he leaned forward. "Tell me about Mack and Remy." Remy Comeaux and Mack Rivet were the two NOPD officers who had worked with him on the Louisiana Disaster Avoidance Task Force Investigations Team back in 2005. "The FBI pulled me out of there so fast once Katrina hit that I wasn't able to contact either of them."

Angel shook her head. "So you didn't know that Lee Barnaby had 'em both arrested—"

"What?" Ray said. "I knew there were some officers who got out of line. But not Mack or Remy. Why in hell would he arrest two of the best cops he—" Ray stopped.

Angel quirked a brow. "Yep. I think you figured out the answer to that one. Probably hoping to shut them up about your sting operation. But I'm guessing Mack's and Remy's files say looting and assault."

Ray was stunned. Mack and Remy were two of the most stand-up guys he'd ever known. His mentor, Mitch Stone at the FBI office in Washington, D.C., had handpicked them to work with Ray on the multiorganizational team to investigate corruption in the LDAT because of their spotless records. They'd been young, like him, but they'd already proved themselves to be detective material.

"I just read something about Barnaby. Wasn't he ousted from his new position as police chief?"

Angel sipped her coffee. "Yep. He's under indictment for corruption and murder. Couldn't have happened to a more deserving guy," she said wryly, then smiled. "That was Remy's doing. Oh, and Mack tracked me down a couple of months ago looking for a hacker. He wanted information about Melvin Landry's financials as well as Mayor Barrow's. Someone had been skimming funds from the city's rebuilding funds and Mack was sure it was Barrow and Landry."

"Melvin Landry. That's Mack's wife's father?"

"Yes. It turned out he was innocent, but Mack was instrumental in bringing down the mayor and Tate Manning, Landry's lawyer, for stealing the city rebuilding funds." Angel looked at her watch. "I've got to get going," Angel said. "I've got a sentencing hearing in an hour."

Ray stood with her. "So Remy and Mack brought down Barnaby and Mayor Barrow."

"You got it," she said with a laugh. "Now, if you can get the goods on Hennessey, we'll have ourselves a Big Easy hat trick."

"That is exactly why I'm here," Ray said, "and why I called you. I need to get in touch with Mack and Remy."

"I've got a phone number for Remy," she said and gave him the information. "Now, seriously, I'm going to be late."

"Okay," he said. He kissed her on the cheek. "Good to see you, and congratulations on the job." He pulled back and looked her in the eye. "One last thing. How in hell does Hennessey, with his history, have the nerve to run for governor?"

Angel straightened her caramel-colored leather jacket and swiped a hand over the sleeked-back hair at her temple. Then she gave Ray an eloquent shrug and shook her head. "What can I say?" she remarked. "This is the Big Easy, *cher.*" She turned and walked toward the door. Ray threw some bills down on the table and followed her.

Outside, she turned to him with a knowing look. "By the way, remember Hennessey's little sister, Molly?" she asked innocently.

Ray swallowed. He wouldn't forget Molly Hennessey if he lived a million years, although he wasn't going to say that to Angel. He'd been undercover as a law student doing an internship with the LDAT over the summer and Molly had been volunteering in her brother's office during her summer vacation from Tulane Law School.

Ray had flirted with her and eventually taken her to bed. He'd gotten what he'd wanted—proof that Hennessey was skimming federal funds. Ray had set up a sting operation to catch Hennessey and several other LDAT officials who were involved, but he'd hurt Molly.

"Ray?" Angel said, snapping her fingers in front of his eyes.

"What? Yeah. Hennessey's little sister," he said flatly.

"Yeah. Martin Hennessey went to work as a real-estate lawyer after Katrina, working with a greasy character who's made a fortune flipping houses and doing who knows what else. Molly took over her brother's law practice when he decided to run for governor."

"Who's the greasy character?"

"Flannery Thrasher. How's that for a ten-dollar name? Get this. He's campaign manager for Hennessey. Word is, he'll be secretary of state when Hennessey wins."

Ray felt relieved. "So at least that means Molly's not working for him."

"That don't mean a thing. Thrasher's with Martin 24/7."

"What are you saying?"

Angel shrugged. "I'm just saying Remy thought you might want to know about him, so I ran him. Turns out I couldn't find a damn thing about Flannery Thrasher before 2005."

Ray frowned. "That's true of a lot of people, isn't it? Weren't hundreds of thousands of documents destroyed in the floods? I lost almost every piece of information I'd collected on the LDAT."

"Sure. But New Orleans vital records for the year of Thrasher's birth are intact, but there's no record of anyone by that name."

"And you did the searches yourself?"

"I damn sure did."

"You mentioned Molly."

Angel checked her watch again. "I met her a couple of times. She seemed like a very sweet girl. But she's surrounded by corruption—her brother, Thrasher, who knows who else. She needs somebody to watch out for her, or she's going to get hurt."

THE NEXT MORNING, Ray sat in the restaurant of the Monteleone hotel looking at the newspaper. The front page had two huge headlines. Most prominent was Hennessey Receives Coveted Endorsement, accompanied by a smiling photo of him and the senior U.S. senator from Louisiana. Slightly smaller and positioned just to the right of Hennessey's photo was the second headline. Does Corruption Extend Beyond Police Department and Mayor's Office?

Ray chuckled, then reached around the paper to pick up his café au lait.

"I had a good laugh when I saw that this morning, too," a familiar voice said from behind him. Remy Comeaux pulled out a chair with one hand and waved the waitress over with the other. He pointed at Ray's mug. She nodded.

Ray set the paper aside. "Good to see you," he said.

Remy eyed him. "Yeah, you, too. Surprised, though. What's the occasion?"

"I just came off a deep undercover assignment and found out that you called the FBI offices looking for me a couple of months ago."

"I wondered why you didn't get back to me," Remy replied. "How deep?"

Ray lifted his mug. "Four years."

"Whoa." Remy shook his head. "Hope it was worth it."

"Yeah." Ray made a dismissive gesture with his hand. "It's over now. I guess you called about Barnaby?"

The waitress set a mug in front of Remy. He nodded his thanks. "That's right. I thought you'd want to know that things had come to a head again after all this time. By the way, Angel said y'all talked yesterday."

"She brought me up-to-date," Ray said.

"I gotta say, it's nice to know all I have to do is pick up the phone and you'll come running," Remy said wryly.

"Anything for you, sweetheart," Ray drawled. "But I didn't come down here because of your phone call—figured you'd already have your problem solved. Before I went undercover, I tried to keep up with what was going on down here, especially with our four friends from LDAT. So when the assignment was over and I got the message that you'd called, I started catching up on everything I'd missed. The first thing I saw was that Hennessey was running for governor."

"Can you believe those bastards came out of Katrina smelling like roses? I was in Houston when I saw that Barnaby had gotten the chief of police position. All I could think was he'd have even more power. So I came back to stop him."

"Good job," Ray said simply. "Why'd you leave in the first place? New Orleans is in your blood."

A shadow crossed Remy's face. "Barnaby threw Mack and me into jail for 'looting.' But the flooding tripped the electronic locks and I just walked out. I went to find Carlotta, but she never showed up at the hospital where she worked. I searched for weeks, but you saw how it was down here, right? So I had to accept that she was gone, along with my job and my city, so I left."

"Oh, man, I am so sorry—" Ray started, but Remy held up his hand, grinning.

"Don't be. Coming back here was the best thing I ever did. I came back looking for Barnaby and I found Carlotta. We're getting married." Remy's normally solemn face glowed.

Ray nodded. "That's great, man. What about Mack?"

"Same song, second verse. He walked out of the jail, too, but I had no idea where he was. Turns out he thought his wife and new baby were dead, too, so he slunk back into the bayou to nurse his wounds. Only, he still got the newspaper, so when Barnaby went down, he contacted me. He was ready to clear our names. He was staking out a party by the local elite and who does he spot alive and well? His wife, Lily. And then he helped bring down more of the players."

"So he ended up proving that Mayor Barrow was in on the government corruption with Barnaby," Ray filled in. "Good job, both of you. Where's Mack now?"

"He and Lily and their son are on a long, quiet vacation at the beach, getting to know each other again."

Ray tapped a finger on the newspaper. "What do you know about Hennessey?"

Remy drained the last of his café au lait and pushed the mug aside. "You mean, can we bring him to the party?" he asked.

Ray nodded. "We had him dead to rights." He held up his closed fist. "We even had a plea agreement with Flay."

"*Had* is right," Remy said with a shake of his head. "Teague Fortune, a detective here in the Sixth, ran Flay for me. There's not a damn thing on him after the storm. No credit cards, no checks. Not even a driver's license or a tax return."

"What does the Department of Public Records do about somebody who just disappears?"

Remy shrugged. "You kidding me? Somebody who disappeared during Katrina? Nothing."

"So you're telling me that Flay is missing and presumed dead?"

"Hell, Ray. It's been eight years. Ain't no presumed about it. Too bad we never had a chance to use that plea bargain."

Ray muttered a few curses he'd learned at his dad's knee. "That sucks. I was counting on Flay's testimony. Most of my evidence was destroyed in the flood. Did you manage to salvage anything?"

Remy shook his head. "Anything that Katrina didn't destroy Barnaby and Barrow got rid of."

"Great," Ray growled. "Hennessey belongs is prison, and I'm planning to put him there. There is no way he's going to be governor if I have anything to say about it."

"Good luck with that. You've only got six months." Remy chuckled.

"Check back with me in six weeks, smart-ass."

"I don't know. You should have seen Hennessey when Barnaby and Barrow went down." Remy punctuated his words by pointing at the picture of Hennessey on the newspaper's front page. "He didn't even blink. He acted as if he didn't even know those two lowlifes. It's like he's made of Teflon."

"We'll see what he's made of. So can I count on you to help me?"

Remy grinned sheepishly. "Love to, Ray, but Carlotta and I are eloping next week. She'll kill me dead if I even look like I want to change our plans."

"Congratulations," Ray said, then added, "Wait a minute. You're planning to elope? Isn't that kind of missing the point?"

"We're getting married in Houston, then flying to Cancun for a week. Want to put all this off for a week or two and go with us?"

"I think I'll stay here and tackle Hennessey. I don't want him to get one millimeter closer to the governor's mansion."

"You call Teague Fortune if you need anything," Remy said. "He's a good guy. Plays his cards close to his chest. You can trust him." Remy gave Ray Fortune's number, then looked at him.

"I wish I could be here, Ray, but true love wins out. Carlotta and I did our part. We took down Barnaby. I'll be back two weeks from today if you need me then." Remy held out his hand. "Good to see you, man."

Ray shook Remy's hand. "Thanks. And thanks for starting the cleanup for me. It'll be easier now that Barnaby and Barrow are out of the way."

"It'll be a banner day when Hennessey goes down. Say—" Remy looked at him "—have you seen his sister, Molly, since you've been here?"

Ray made a show of getting out his wallet. "Nope. I just got here yesterday."

"You ought to check on her," Remy said. "She was nice. Too bad she's got a son of a bitch for a brother." He touched his forefinger to his temple. "Call me if there's anything I can help you with *over the phone.*"

Ray smiled. "Will do. Thanks, Remy."

After Remy left, Ray stared at Hennessey's photo. Ray had been the only one on the investigative team who'd actually worked at the LDAT offices. He'd never told Remy or Mack about Molly or what he'd done, although they knew that Hennessey's cute college-age sister was volunteering at her brother's office. He'd never told them how he knew about the secret meeting called by Hennessey to plan the diversion of grant moneys. Afterward, when the planning meeting turned out to be a poker game, and Mack had casually mentioned Hennessey's sister and suggested that pillow talk was never reliable, Ray had clenched his jaw and kept his mouth shut.

He didn't have to be told that it was his fault Hennessey, Barnaby and Barrow had come through Katrina smelling like roses. Or that he was responsible for Remy and Mack losing eight years of their lives. Bringing Hennessey down would go a long way toward making it up to both of them.

Right now, though, two people had said he needed to check on Molly, and that was exactly what he was going to do.

Chapter Two

That afternoon, Ray was loitering across Canal Street from the building that housed the Hennessey law offices when Molly Hennessey walked out through the tall glass doors and turned left on Canal. She had on a short, flouncy skirt and platform heels. From his vantage point, her legs were just as long and toned and the rest of her just as slender and perfect as he remembered.

As he watched, she stopped at the corner, checked the Walk/Don't Walk sign, sent a hurried glance up and down the street, then ran across to the neutral ground barely in time to miss the traffic.

Ray took a deep breath and stuck his phone into his pocket. He arched his neck, plastered a *Me? I'm just walking down the street* look on his face and set off on a collision course with her. He walked as if he hadn't a care in the world.

Just as the light changed and Molly headed across, Ray caught a glimpse of a man he'd noticed earlier hanging around the attorneys' building. The man lumbered awkwardly into the neutral ground. Soft and sweaty, with thinning wisps of brown hair blowing straight back as he stumbled up onto the curb, he was hardly noticeable—unless you knew him.

And Ray knew him, although he couldn't think of his name. Before Katrina, he'd been a two-bit private detective who'd done some quasi-legal work for Patrick Flay. There was no way it was a coincidence that he was tailing Molly.

Ray slowed his pace, grabbed his phone and snapped a couple of shots of the P.I. Just as he finished, he ran smack into Molly as she hopped up onto the sidewalk.

"Oh," she cried as her purse hit the sidewalk upside down and the contents spilled everywhere. "Oh, no!"

Ray dropped to his haunches and snagged several escaping

pennies, dimes and quarters. Molly crouched, too, balancing precariously on the platform heels. She grabbed the purse and righted it, shoveling as much back into it as she could.

"Sorry," Ray muttered, not sorry at all. He hadn't meant for her purse to spill—hadn't meant to literally run into her, but it was better than the clumsy, choreographed collision and fake apology he'd planned. He picked up a lip gloss that rolled to rest against the toe of his shoe. The tube was pink with red letters proclaiming *Sweetest Strawberry*.

He stared at it, then at her lips. So that was why she'd always tasted like that. A scent memory fed him flashes of them kissing and laughing and rolling around in bed. A spear of lust hit him in the groin. He groaned.

Molly lifted her head and he fell right into her dark eyes, just as he had the first time he'd met her. He swallowed and dragged his gaze away from hers, quickly checking on the P.I. The man was waiting for the light to change with his phone next to his ear. He spoke urgently as he squinted at the two of them. When he realized Ray was looking at him, he glanced behind him, as if considering retreating. But he stayed put. *Barny.* The lowlife's name was Barny Acles.

Ray turned back to Molly as her expression morphed from blank through surprise to irritation. Her head jerked slightly backward and she wavered on those silly heels.

"Ray?" she whispered, her face blanching. Then she shook her head and laughed shortly. "Sorry," she said, closing her purse and rising. "For a moment there, I thought you looked familiar." She slung the straps of her purse over her shoulder and smoothed the front of her skirt.

Ray stood, too. "Hi, Molly," he said lightly. "Sorry about—" He gestured vaguely.

"Ray?" This time the word came out as a hoarse whisper. "Ray Storm?" She looked up at him as if working to convince herself that her vision wasn't playing tricks on her.

He nodded, smiling. But inside, he steeled himself. As soon as she decided that it really was him, she was going to do one of two things: slap him or turn on her heel and walk away. Hell, she'd probably do both. "It's me."

She shook her head and kept on shaking it—slowly and steadily. She took a step backward and angled her head. He watched a muscle twitch in her jaw. Her pale skin began to regain its color, starting with splotches of pink in her cheeks. "So you're not dead," she said tightly. "I should have known."

He held his breath. This was the deciding moment. To his surprise, she didn't slap him. She merely executed a spectacular pirouette and walked away.

"Molly, wait." He reached for her arm.

She jerked away and squared her shoulders. That gave him enough time to jump in front of her. "Come on, Molly. Let's talk. Catch up."

She whirled back to face him, the sudden dampness in her eyes catching the late-afternoon sun. He felt a pang in his chest.

"Catch up?" she echoed. "No. I don't want to *catch up* with you. So if you didn't die, I guess that means you just up and left. Went back to wherever it was your family lived. It must have been nice to have someplace to go to escape the *inconvenience* of Katrina."

She swiped at her cheeks. "I'm not crying about you," she said defiantly, her chin going up another millimeter. "It's just—even after eight years, I still hear about someone I knew who died in the flooding. Or somebody I thought was dead shows up."

That last had a bitter flavor to it.

She gestured, open-handed, toward her eyes. "It's kind of an emotional roller coaster."

"Let me buy you a cup of coffee," he tried.

She glared at him. "Congratulations on living through the storm, Ray Storm." With that, she turned on her heel and flounced off.

Ray watched her until she entered a drugstore. Then he looked back at the neutral ground, but Acles had disappeared.

MOLLY HENNESSEY CLOSED the front door behind her and took a deep, shaky breath. She set the bag from the drugstore on the kitchen counter along with her purse, then held out her hands and watched them quiver.

Ray Storm was the last person in the world she'd expected to see today—or ever. She still had nightmares about the last time she'd seen him—the day before the storm. The day she'd realized that the only reason he'd slept with her was to get evidence that her brother was skimming federal grant moneys from the Louisiana Disaster Avoidance Task Force, or LDAT. Stupidly, she'd given him every last bit of information she'd known.

She hadn't heard a word from or about Ray since Katrina. She hadn't lied when she'd said she'd thought he was dead. In the chaos that reigned once the flooding started, thousands of people were left wondering about friends, neighbors and family. A significant fraction hadn't made it. She'd grieved for Ray until anger finally replaced the sadness. Anger at him for using her teenage rebelliousness and her self-righteous outrage at her brother's thievery to get evidence against him. Anger at him for making her fall in love with him.

No. Not in love. She shook her head as she headed for her bedroom to change, kicking off the heels. It had been a hard lesson to learn at age eighteen that the man she'd given her virginity to had used her to get proof of the discrepancies she'd found between funds received and funds used for the LDAT program. Once he had them, he was practically out the door.

Then, as soon as Katrina had hit, he'd disappeared. She'd feared the worst. Now she knew. Of course he hadn't died. He'd just escaped back to wherever he'd come from. He'd deserted New Orleans. He'd deserted her. He didn't deserve her love.

But damn, he'd looked great today. Really great. Same thick black hair, same dangerously dark eyes and the same crooked smile that had never once failed to melt her heart. His lanky body had filled out in the past eight years. He was still lean, but in a hard, silk-over-steel, grown-up way.

Then he'd had the gall to offer her a cup of coffee—to *catch up*. Catch up! Like coworkers who'd lost touch. Her fingers curled into claws. If she had a do-over and longer fingernails, she'd claw his eyes out for walking out on the devastation and sadness of the storm. For walking out on her.

She closed her eyes and tried to banish that first shock of recognition when she'd looked up from her spilled purse. But the darkness behind her closed lids made a nice canvas on which to display his handsome face.

It had taken her a long time to get over his callous betrayal. She'd been only eighteen. He'd been her first lover. She remembered the tender surprise and chagrin on his face when he'd realized that.

She'd grown up a lot during the past eight years. She'd dated some pretty fine men, but no matter how much she cared about them, she'd never been able to commit to the long haul. The memory of Ray's crooked, dimpled grin always got in the way.

Okay. That was enough thinking about Ray Storm. It was Wednesday night and she had a date—with herself—to watch her favorite cooking competition show. She needed something for dinner that was portable, satisfying and yet with zero calories. That was the only way she'd fit into the red designer dress she planned to wear to her brother Martin's $500-a-plate gubernatorial campaign kickoff dinner on Friday night.

Just as she opened the refrigerator to check if the lettuce in her crisper had turned to slime, her doorbell rang. Frowning, she glanced up at the kitchen clock. It was after 7:00 p.m. She rolled her eyes. It was probably some kids selling candy for a school fundraiser or hawking subscriptions to the daily paper.

She went to the door and looked through the peephole but saw nothing. She put the chain on and opened the door a crack. "Yes?" she said, letting impatience tinge her tone.

"Molly, hi."

The familiar voice sent a shiver up her spine. It was Ray. How had he gotten her address? As soon as the question flitted through her mind, she berated herself for her stupidity. He was an FBI agent. He probably had a file with everything from the address of her first-grade teacher to the date of her last period.

"What are you doing here?" she asked tiredly.

"Open up. I need to talk to you."

She peered through the tiny opening allowed by the chain. He was standing a nonthreatening foot and a half away from the door. "I'm not dressed."

That crooked smile raised the corners of his mouth. "Ha. That shouldn't be a problem. From what I remember, you probably have two closets full of clothes in there."

"Bite me," she said and pushed the door closed. But she didn't walk away. Her mistake.

"Molly, please."

Her heart gave a little jump. He'd closed that nonthreatening eighteen inches by at least twelve. It sounded as though he'd put his mouth to the crack between the door and the facing.

"This is important. I need to let you know about something."

With a sigh she opened the door again, to the width allowed by the chain. "Tell me," she said.

"Come on, Mols. Let me in. I promise I'll be good."

"I swear, Ray, if this is a trick of some kind—"

"It's not."

She heard the serious tone in his voice. "Come in and close the door. I'll be right back. I'm going to get dressed."

He stepped inside. "Don't bother. This isn't going to take but a minute. Besides," he continued, eyeing her from head to toe and back up again, "you're more covered up than you were this afternoon. That skirt couldn't have been more than eighteen inches long."

She compressed her lips. "If you're claiming to be the fashion police, I'll need to see your badge."

He shook his head, his mouth quirking in that smile. "I'll be serious."

"Fine," she said, crossing her arms. "What is it?"

"Are you aware that you're being followed?" he asked.

"What?" Molly wasn't sure what she'd expected, but it sure hadn't been that. "Followed? By whom? Other than you, that is." She sent him a look designed to let him know she hadn't been fooled by their accidental meeting.

He inclined his head, acknowledging the truth of her statement. "Okay, I deserved that. But I swear, you're being tailed.

The guy is a P.I. who has apparently moved *way* up in the world since Katrina. Back then his targets were generally found sneaking around cheap motel rooms."

"Ray—" she said warningly.

"His name is Barny Acles. I saw him this afternoon when I ran into you."

She lifted her chin. "What made you think he's following me?"

"He was right behind you crossing Canal, and I think he recognized me. That should have made him back off, but it didn't. At least not right away."

"Why?"

"He used to do some work for Patrick Flay. So he knows who I am."

She rolled her eyes. "I meant why is he following me?"

"Hell if I know. Would your brother put a tail on you?"

"My brother trusts me," she said, suddenly hit by the memory of the last time she'd seen Ray. Her brother had trusted her then, too, but she'd nearly betrayed him.

"What about safety?" Ray asked. "Although, I'd think Martin Hennessey would want someone better than Acles if his purpose was to keep his baby sister safe."

"Martin is not worried about me. He announced his candidacy back in January and it's March now. I've been safe so far."

Ray nodded, looking thoughtful. "Maybe he received a threat against you. Maybe it's the incumbent, hoping to get something on you so he can knock Martin out of the race."

"Something on *me?*" She laughed. "You know that's not going to happen."

He grinned, exposing that dimple in his right cheek, and her heart skipped a beat. She hadn't meant to draw him in with a shared memory. It was too intimate. Sadly, he had known her well enough to know that there was nothing anyone could *get* on her. Even sadder, he knew that it was still true, even after eight years. "How do you know this P.I.?" she asked.

"He's one of the few things that hasn't changed a bit around here in the past eight years. He's still as sneaky and doughy as he was before Katrina."

"Doughy?" she echoed.

"You know, soft and pudgy and sweaty."

"Oh," she said, sidling toward the front door. She needed him to leave. His tall, lanky frame filled up her house. He was too tall, too good-looking and too sexy. The longer he stayed, the less she'd be able to resist him.

Ray watched Molly as she moved around him toward the door. As she slid sideways, doing her best not to touch him, the edges of the kimono separated a little and he caught a glimpse of her bare leg from toe all the way past the top of her thigh to the small bump of her hipbone.

Suddenly, he couldn't think straight. He blinked and tried to drag his gaze away. He really did. But her skin looked as creamy and firm as it had eight years ago. What he'd said to her about her clothes had been technically correct—the long kimono did cover a larger percentage of her body than the short skirt and blouse she'd had on earlier. But there was a big difference between an outfit suitable for appearing in public and a garment that could get her arrested for indecent exposure. Indecent but tantalizing exposure, he amended as he noted the outline of her nipples through the thin silk and, by using very little imagination, the subtle V at the apex of her thighs. A gnawing hunger to see more left his mouth as dry as the Sahara and his body tensed against his rising desire.

"Thanks for the info," she said with a definite chill in her voice as she wrapped the kimono more tightly around her. "I'll tell Martin about the guy. Acles, right?"

With a lot more willpower than he'd have thought he possessed, he turned toward the door and put his hand on the knob. But then he paused. *No time like the present,* he thought with a pang of regret. *Might as well burn this bridge now as later.*

He hadn't meant to blurt out that she was being followed. He had come to warn her, but he could have handled it more delicately. Especially since he didn't know where the danger was coming from. His best bet was that Acles had been hired by her brother, Martin Hennessey.

"Molly, I'd like to talk to you for a minute."

She sighed. "You've *been* talking. And believe me, I appreciate the info. I'll sleep better tonight knowing that there's a pudgy, pasty P.I. following me," she drawled. She made an *after you* gesture toward the door.

Ray didn't miss the irony in her tone. She didn't like him, and he couldn't blame her. He'd betrayed her trust and taken advantage of her naïveté. "No matter what you think of me, no matter how much it hurts you, you know I was right about Martin," he said, figuring he might as well dive in headfirst. He was already up to his butt in alligators, as the saying went. "Even without the evidence from the meeting that Sunday night, I had enough to bring your brother and the others before the grand jury. You didn't need me to tell you that your brother was involved in something illegal. You'd already made those copies of the financial papers with huge discrepancies and the memos that proved Martin was in it up to his neck. Have you forgotten that you gave me copies?"

She closed her eyes. "No, I haven't forgotten. But Martin's different now. He got married after Katrina. They're separated right now, but I'm hoping they can work it out. He has a little boy—my nephew." Her eyes lit up and her voice was filled with pride. "My brother has done a lot of good for New Orleans these past eight years. He has set up grants and loans for local businesses to get back on their feet. He's acquired federal funding for rebuilding in the flooded areas—"

Ray stared at her.

"Don't say it, Ray," she said quickly, waving her hand. "There's no way he's involved in skimming moneys these days. He's running for governor!"

"Right. The only reason he's free to do that is because of a natural disaster. He'd be in prison now if Katrina hadn't hit. If the levees hadn't broken—"

Molly laughed. "You sound like my granddad. 'If we had some ham, we could have ham and eggs—if we had some eggs. In other words, you've got nothing.'"

"You know my evidence was solid. Recording that Sunday night meeting would have been the icing on the cake. It would have saved the prosecution a lot of time by proving that your brother, Barnaby, Barrow and Flay all knew the same things."

"You keep talking about the evidence. If you've got enough to take my brother down, where is it?"

He grimaced. "You know the answer to that. My hard drive was practically irretrievable. The printouts, including the copies you gave me, were completely destroyed by the water and mud."

"So in fact, you really don't have any evidence."

"All I've got is what I'd already transferred to Washington and the record of Flay's plea bargain." He shrugged. "And that's worth zilch if Flay's dead. You, on the other hand, have more than enough to put your brother in prison."

She stared at him. "Me? I don't know what you mean," she said levelly.

"Come on, Molly. Are you telling me you didn't keep copies of those financial statements? Or the memos with margin notes that incriminate your brother?" He shook his head. "I don't buy it. You haven't changed that much."

She shook her head, looking a bit shell-shocked. She opened her mouth, then closed it again.

Ray watched her struggle with her conscience. Of course she had the papers. He could tell by her face that she was trying to figure out how to lie. Truth was, she was a terrible liar.

"Martin is my brother," she said finally. "I was only nine years old when our parents died. He's been my only family my whole life. I'm not going to help you ruin him."

"Not even if his election means more years of diverted funds? Funds that could prevent another disaster like Katrina, that could put food in the mouths of needy children, that could—"

"Stop it! You can't know that! You're trying to manipulate me again. I'm not that naive girl anymore."

Ray winced. "Look. I can't deny that I was a jerk back then. It was wrong of me to—"

"To what, Ray? Seduce me? Take advantage of the poor young thing? Don't flatter yourself," she said, her cheeks turning pink. "You weren't all that. Contrary to what your ego and libido think, I knew what I was doing."

He raised his hands, palms out. "Okay. I apologize." He shrugged. "I apologize for not trying to find you before I had to leave. I apologize if I hurt you." He looked down for a split second. "I apologize for using you to get to your brother. I don't blame you for telling him his office was bugged."

"Telling him—" Molly stared at him. "What are you talking about? I didn't tell him."

"What? Come on. It had to be you. Nobody else knew. Have you forgotten where we were when I let it slip that we were planning to raid that Sunday night meeting?" He certainly hadn't. He had erotic dreams of lying with her in the single bed in her tiny bedroom of the off-campus apartment she shared with three other girls. Laughing and making love from Friday night until Sunday afternoon, when she'd finally begged him to leave so she could study.

"No," she said. "I haven't forgotten. But please. What about the other people on *your* team?"

"The people on my team were police officers."

"And therefore above reproach. Seriously?"

"I can guarantee you that neither of them gave up our plan."

"Well, I can guarantee you that I didn't."

Ray studied her. He'd known her for about eight weeks during the summer of 2005, while he was working hard to make a success of his first undercover operation as an FBI agent and get proof to bring down three prominent officials. But as short a time as that was, he was confident that he knew her well enough to be sure she wasn't lying.

So the question remained, if she hadn't outed him to her brother, who had? He filed that question away for another time. Right now he needed what only she had, and he wasn't looking forward to asking for it.

"Molly, I need those papers."

"What papers?"

"You know what papers. The ones you copied for me. The ones that implicate your brother."

The light that always shone from her eyes went out. "That's why you're here."

He gritted his teeth and forced himself to hold her gaze. "It's not the only reason."

She laughed. "Please. Even if I were still eighteen, I'd have sense enough to know that you didn't just wake up one morning and think, 'Hey, it's been eight years. I wonder how Molly is.'"

"Mols—"

"Don't. Assuming I even have the papers, if it were my last day on earth and my brother had murdered half the population of New Orleans, I wouldn't give them to you. Now, get out of my house."

"Come on, Mols, you did the right thing back then."

She lifted her chin and eyed him narrowly. "Back then, I made my decision for all the wrong reasons. I was blinded by a silly schoolgirl crush." She propped her hands on her hips. "I know better now. Please leave."

Chapter Three

First thing the next morning, Ray called Teague Fortune.

"Where y'at?" Teague said. Ray was familiar enough with Cajun slang to understand that the phrase was a greeting, not an actual question. "Remy said you wanted to know about some guy name of Patrick Flay."

"That's right," Ray said.

"Here we go," Teague continued. "After Katrina, Patrick Flay's car was found on Elysian Fields Avenue out in Gentilly, upside down, and there was no sign of Flay's body."

"Any indication of what happened? Did the car turn over there, or was it carried there by the floodwaters? And where did Flay live?"

"Residence, 4478 Touro Street. Touro's off Elysian Fields, and that whole area was underwater. So I can't tell you where the car turned over. He could have been trying to get home or trying to get out."

"What about his bank accounts? What about his family?"

"I don't have anything but police records. I'll have to check out the other records. Give me a few days."

"Thanks."

"Sounds to me like you don't think Patrick Flay is dead."

"My job would be a whole lot easier if he wasn't, since there's no statute of limitations on a plea agreement."

"You got that right, I guarantee. You find Flay, you take down Hennessey. *C'est finis.*"

As soon as he hung up, Ray headed down to the French Quarter. If he remembered correctly, Acles perched down here somewhere on the edge of the Quarter, where drug dealers, addicts and two-bit whores lurked out of reach of the bright lights of the more insulated center streets. Down there, quaint, picturesque and fabulous could turn into creepy, dirty and dangerous from one side of a street to another. Acles's office was definitely on the wrong side of the street.

Ray walked down Decatur and turned left on Urselines. About three-quarters of the way to Rampart, he saw a tiny, peeling sign. Barnabus Acles Investigations.

He touched the paddle holster at the small of his back where his SIG Sauer was tucked, shrugged to settle his summer-weight jacket onto his shoulders and stepped through the narrow door. The foyer was dark and narrow. Squinting, he spotted a piece of paper taped to the wall. An arrow pointed up the stairs and the name ACLES was printed in block letters.

Feeling sweat beginning to run down his back, Ray climbed the stairs cautiously. When he checked out the second floor, he found a second scrap of paper with the same writing on it. Behind the door he heard a TV. He knocked and listened. There was a soft thud and a squeaking noise like the springs on an old office chair. Ray took a step backward.

Acles opened the door, pushing his thinning hair back from his sweat-drenched forehead.

"Oh," the P.I. said when he met Ray's gaze. "It's you. You know, it's still a free country. You can't do anything to me for walking on Canal Street."

"You can walk anywhere you damn well please as long as you stop tailing Molly Hennessey."

Acles shook his head. "Who?"

"Give me a break, Acles. Who's paying you to follow her?"

"I got no idea what you're talking about." Acles tried to close the door but Ray stopped it with one hand.

"Hey," Acles snapped. "You got no—"

"Can it, Acles. Who hired you? And I'm warning you, in about five seconds I'm going to smash your nose if you don't start talking."

"Nope," Acles said, his words sounding braver than he looked. "I can't violate client privilege."

Ray laughed. "You're invoking sleazy P.I./client privilege?"

The P.I.'s face turned beet-red. He muttered a vile curse. "I'm invoking *no dice.*" He tried to shove the door closed again.

Ray shot out an arm and grabbed his shirt collar. He lifted the P.I. off the ground and got in his face. "How about the I-can-beat-you-up clause?" Ray said, his teeth bared in a grimace. For all his pasty softness, the P.I. was heavy.

Acles, struggling to stay on his tiptoes, choked out, "Okay, okay."

Ray loosened his grip on his shirt collar and the man stumbled backward until he hit his desk.

"Ow!" he yelled. "Watch out. You could have broke my back."

"With all the insulation you've got? I doubt it. Now, who. Hired. You. To. Tail. Molly?" Ray repeated. "And why?"

"Okay, okay, I don't know, I swear," Acles said. "I got the gig by phone—couldn't run a trace on it. Burner phone, I guess."

"Is it Martin Hennessey?"

The P.I.'s beady eyes went wide. "Her brother?" he exclaimed, shaking his head. "No. I mean, how would I know?"

"Right. How would you? It was just a voice on the phone. You just take any low-down job that somebody will pay you for?" Ray said distastefully.

Acles blinked as a drop of sweat dripped into his eye. He thumbed it away. "Well, yeah," he said. "I mean, money is money."

Ray suppressed a shudder. *Money is money.* He'd heard those words too many times from his dad growing up. He wanted to punch Acles in the mouth for reminding him. "Yeah?" he grated through clenched teeth. "I hope you bought yourself a good dental plan, because in about two minutes you're going to need a lot of work done."

Acles cowered backward, holding a hand up to shield his mouth. "The message is on my phone." Acles grabbed the phone from his desk and handed it to Ray. Ray pocketed it.

"Hey!" Acles started. "That's my—"

"It's evidence now."

"Evidence? Of what? You don't have anything on me." Acles's voice quavered.

Ray ignored him. "Whose voice is it?"

Acles's face drained of color. "I swear, man. I can't. I don't—" The rest of that sentence was choked off as Ray took two steps, reached across the desk and grabbed Acles's shirt collar again.

He dragged the P.I. halfway across the desk. "I need answers. How do you want me to get them?" He tightened his grip on Acles's collar.

The man coughed and flailed his arms. "Okay! Let—me go! I'll tell you," he panted.

Ray loosened his hold and the other man flopped down onto the table.

Acles struggled to his feet, breathing heavily. "It could be Hennessey," he panted. "I mean, I couldn't swear to it, but it could be."

"You little worm," Ray said disgustedly. "Sending me on a wild-goose chase isn't going to help you. I'll just come back mad as hell. Now, try to tell me the truth for a change. How're you supposed to report to whoever hired you? And how do you get your money?"

"There's a guy on Tchoupitoulas runs a message service. You pay to leave a message. More if you want the guy to call and let somebody know they've got a message waiting."

"And the recipient doesn't pay anything. Right." Ray knew all about those places. In New York, back when he was a kid, barely old enough to understand that what his dad did was illegal, Ray had made runs to the message service for him.

"I've dealt with places like that. Nobody uses their real name and everything is cash only. You listen to me, you worthless—" Ray stopped, pulling in a deep breath. "You're working for me now. First, I want you to keep following Molly. Second, if anything—and I mean anything—starts to go down involving Molly, you call me, and if you have to, call 911. Because if something happens to her, you're going to get it back quadruple. Got it?"

"The police? I can't— I mean—" Acles stepped backward and his back hit the wall of the tiny cubicle.

"You can and you will, if you know what's good for you."

"They'll kill me."

"Don't worry. I'll kill you, too, if anything happens to Molly." Ray took a deep breath. "Third, I want you to find out who ordered Molly followed."

Acles started shaking his head. "I don't ask no questions," he whined. "That way I don't know nothing when it all goes down."

Ray ignored him. "Write this down," he commanded and watched as Acles fumbled for a pencil and a piece of paper. When the P.I. was finally ready, Ray gave him his number.

"But you took my phone," Acles whined.

Ray reached into his pocket for his wallet and peeled off two twenties. "Here," he said, tossing them down on the desk amid all the clutter. "Get yourself a new one."

Acles eyed the money but didn't move.

"One last question. Where's Patrick Flay?" The P.I.'s eye's flickered.

"I—I think he died in Katrina," he stammered.

Ray grabbed a fistful of sweat-drenched shirt collar. "You're a damned pathetic liar, Acles."

"I swear," Acles croaked. "I swear! Far as I know, nobody's seen nor heard from him since then, but—" He coughed. "I'm choking, man," he rasped.

Ray let go of him. "But what?"

"That message service? It's the same one Flay used—you know—before. But I swear I never heard that voice before."

Acles coughed again.

"Okay," Ray said. He had the feeling this time the man was telling the truth. He leaned across the desk to get in the guy's face. "Don't forget who you're working for. Who are you working for?"

"You," Acles panted.

"I'll be waiting to hear from you." With that, Ray left, taking the narrow stairs down two at a time. He felt vaguely nauseous. He'd been too close to that lowlife for too long. Dealing with scum like Acles—and worse—was a major reason he'd left home at seventeen and worked his way through college. Despite, or maybe because of, the influence of his dad and brother, he'd always wanted to be a cop. Sometimes he still had nightmares about what his life would have been like if he hadn't gotten away. His older brother, Shane, had dropped out of high school to follow in their dad's footsteps. Until that time, Ray had idolized his older brother and wanted to be just like him.

Shane's decision cemented Ray's determination to *catch* the bad guys, not be one of them.

IT WAS AFTER NINE when Molly turned left onto her street. She was tired and it didn't help that her brother was being his usual pompous self. She turned down the volume on her car's Bluetooth as the sound of Martin shuffling papers came through the phone.

"Why on earth would you ask me a question like that?" he asked.

Molly rolled her eyes. He was sixteen years older than she—old enough to be her father. In fact, after their mother and father died in a car wreck when Molly was nine, Martin had taken care of her.

She loved him dearly, but when he talked to her as though she were still nine years old, she wanted to choke him. He talked to everybody that way, but being his baby sister, Molly had endured it for a lifetime.

"I keep seeing this guy everywhere I go," she replied. "Maybe it's nothing." What she meant was maybe she shouldn't have brought it up until Ray got back to her with more information. If he was planning to.

"I don't understand. Out of all the people walking on Canal at rush hour, you noticed this one guy. Is he cute?"

"I'm not twelve, Martin. No. He's not cute. He's creepy. I didn't just *notice* him. I've seen him several times." A small lie, but Ray had been certain the man was following her.

"What does he look like?"

Molly thought about Ray's description. "Pasty, sweaty, thinning hair." She shrugged. "Average, I guess."

She heard a pen scratching. "Okay," Martin said. "I'll check into it for you."

"I didn't ask you to check into it. I asked you if you hired him to follow me."

He sighed and she felt his disapproval through the phone. "That's a disingenuous question," he said dismissively. "Now, I'm busy, so if there's nothing else—"

She sighed and shook her head. "And *that* is no answer. This is not a political debate. You *may* answer honestly," she said sarcastically as she turned onto her street.

"Molly, be rational. Why would I hire someone to follow you?"

"It's not like you don't have enemies. The incumbent governor for one. Or, let's see. Maybe you're worried about my safety."

"Your safety—" He interrupted himself with a chuckle. "You're perfectly safe. Why wouldn't you be?"

"Or maybe you think I might do something to embarrass you."

"That possibility has existed for years," he said with a smile in his voice. Such statements were the closest he got to humor. "I have no recollection of ever seeing a person matching the description you gave."

Molly rolled her eyes. "Spoken like a true politician. I don't suppose I could get a simple yes or no out of you, could I?"

"No," he said shortly.

Another lame joke. He was really feeling his oats today. "Oh, ha-ha. Funny," she responded drolly.

"I'm busy, so if there's nothing else—"

"Martin, are you having me followed or not?" she demanded as she pulled into her driveway. There was a slight pause on the other end of the phone, almost undetectable. Just enough to make her suspicious.

"Molly, I can assure you—" He stopped. "Oh, Flan," he said, his voice changing. "I didn't hear you come in. Molly, Flan's here and we need to go over my speech for the campaign kickoff dinner this week. I'll have to talk to you later."

Molly gritted her teeth. It didn't matter what Martin was doing. Even playing with Benjamin, his four-year-old son, if Thrasher showed up, Martin dropped everything. It was one of the many things Molly couldn't stand about Flannery Thrasher.

And she suspected it was the main reason Jan had taken Benjamin and left Martin.

"Fine, then," she said shortly. "I have no choice but to assume you put the guy on my tail."

"I have to go," Martin repeated. "Call me."

"Of course," she said wryly. "If you can squeeze me in during the five minutes Thrasher's not there monopolizing your time." She hung up, her head filled with an endless supply of better retorts to her brother's flaccid comments than she'd been able to think of at the time. She unlocked her front door and went inside. She set her purse and keys down on the kitchen counter, then stopped and looked at them thoughtfully.

Something wasn't right. Had the key turned too easily in the front door? She glanced around the kitchen, then turned to look back at the door. Briefly, she wondered if she should go outside and get into her car, then call the police. If she did, what would she tell them? That her house didn't feel right? Right.

As she headed down the hall to her bedroom, she noticed that the door to the guest bedroom, which also served as her office, was open. Hadn't she closed it last night? Automatically, she reached around, turning on the lights.

While she did, somebody grabbed her arm. With a small shriek, she recoiled, but the hand was too strong. It jerked her forward so hard and fast that she lost her footing and fell. Her head glanced off the corner of the brass bed, stunning her. With fireworks going off behind her eyes, she collapsed in a heap on the floor.

Chapter Four

The next thing Molly knew, a cold piece of steel was pressed against her temple and a voice was talking to her in a raspy whisper. "Where are the papers?"

She tried to push herself up to her hands and knees so she could sit up, but a heavy hand shoved her down again.

"The papers," he said.

"What?" she croaked as the cold circle of steel pressed harder against her temple.

"The papers, bitch. And we know you've got 'em. Sad day when a brother can't trust his own little sister to keep his secrets, ain't it?"

"Who—are you?" she groaned. "Did Martin send you?"

"Shut up!" the voice growled. "Where are they, *Molly?*"

The way he said her name made her shiver.

She struggled to move. "I don't know," she cried, then sucked in air, prepared to scream.

"Don't be stupid, bitch." This time he grabbed the back of her head. "I can break your nose," he threatened.

She froze.

He moved the gun's barrel from her temple to her cheek. "Or—I can shoot this so it doesn't kill you," he said. "Think about it. The bullet'll go through your cheeks, probably shoot your tongue off, maybe even your nose."

She felt sick. She tried to swallow but her mouth was too dry. "No," she whispered hoarsely. "The safe—in the closet. Th-the combination is—" For a terrifying second, she couldn't remember. Tears welled in her eyes. "It's ninety—no, wait. It's fifteen, ninety-two, el-eleven."

He let go of her and took two steps over to her closet.

"Just take everything and go, please," she begged, hating herself for crouching there, too frightened to run, but knowing she was helpless against a man with a gun.

After a few fumbles, punctuated with colorful curses, he finally got the door open. Papers rustled, then he groaned as he stood. "Is this everything?"

"Wh-what?" she stammered stupidly.

"Answer me!" he yelled and kicked her halfheartedly in the ribs.

"Oof," she groaned. "Yes—" She knew he hadn't kicked hard, but his shoes were heavy and they hurt.

He grabbed her hair and lifted her head, not enough that she could see his face, but enough to make tears spring to her eyes. He leaned in close and she felt his sweat drip onto her cheek and neck. "Now, are you going to lie still like a good little girl, or do I need to knock you out?"

She tried to shake her head, but his grip on her hair was too tight. He lifted her head a little higher. She did her best to blink away tears and try to see something from the corner of her eye at least. More of his sweat dripped onto her face. "I'll lie st-still," she whispered. "I swear. Just please don't hurt me."

He laughed, a surprisingly squeaky, high-pitched sound. "No problem if these are all of 'em. They *are* all of 'em, right?"

"Y-yes." The angle of her head put a lot of pressure on her throat, and she had the urge to cough. She gave in to it, gasping and hacking. He let go of her hair and she collapsed to the floor, still hacking.

Then he was gone. His heavy footsteps reverberated on the hardwood floors. Then the front door banged against the wall. Molly didn't move for a long time. She just lay there, breathing shallowly through her mouth as she listened, terrified that he would come back.

Finally, feeling like a coward, she curled up into a little ball and cried.

RAY FOUND THE MESSAGE SERVICE on Tchoupitoulas Avenue, but as he'd predicted, he got very little from the Asian man who sat behind an old wooden desk. All he got was that the box hadn't been used since Hurricane Katrina. He mentally filed that information away, although he had little hope that it would be useful.

Then he drove over to Molly's. He'd promised himself he'd check on her every day. He turned onto her street in time to see a junker car peeling away from the curb at the corner. Some kid hoping to impress his girlfriend, he figured.

Ray parked across the street from Molly's house, idly wondering why she had so many lights on. Maybe he'd spooked her by telling her about Acles. He wasn't going to worry her even more by letting her know he was watching her house. He'd stick around for an hour or so just to make sure everything was all right. If some hypervigilant husband and father came out to see why he was parked on a quiet street after dark, he'd just drive off.

He watched the house for a few minutes, but despite the lights, he saw no signs of life. He shifted in the driver's seat and looked up and down the street. Everything seemed prefectly normal. And yet, every instinct told him something was wrong.

He argued with himself. She could be reading or watching TV. It was almost nine-thirty. She could be in the shower. But even while he tried to convince himself there was nothing wrong, he got out of his car, walked across the street and up onto her porch. When he raised his hand to knock on her door, he saw that it was slightly ajar. He pushed against it with his knuckles and it swung open.

He froze, not breathing as he glanced around Molly's living room. Everything looked just as it had earlier, except that Molly wasn't there. He drew his weapon and stepped into the living room and shut the door behind him.

"Mols?" he called softly. "It's Ray. Are you here?"

No answer. He moved forward, leading with his weapon, until he could see into the kitchen. "Molly?" he called a little louder. Her purse was on the counter along with her car keys, but again there was no sign of her.

"Molly! It's Ray," he said, raising his voice again. He turned toward the hall that led to the bedrooms. There was a piece of paper lying on the floor near the wall. He stepped over to pick it up. And that was when he heard the sound.

Small, barely audible. It sounded like crying. His hand reflexively tightened around his gun's handle. His finger hovered over the trigger. He shifted to the balls of his feet, ready for anything. Carefully, silently, he crept down the hall.

He glanced into Molly's empty bedroom, then turned toward the other room. The door was half-shut. He reached around the facing and turned on the bedroom light. In the first bright split second, he took in the ransacked room, the tossed drawers and closet, and Molly lying on the floor in a crumpled heap. As soon as the light came on, she jerked and tried to scream, but the only sound that escaped her throat was a rasping, wordless cry.

"Molly!"

"No!" she croaked. "There's nothing else!"

"Molly. It's Ray!" He touched her shoulder.

"No!" she cried again, then froze. Her head came up slowly. "R-Ray?" she whispered. "Oh, my God, Ray." She tried to sit up.

Immediately he pulled back. What the hell was he thinking? "Molly, don't move. Are you okay?"

She shook her head, and when she looked up at him, he saw abject fear in her red, teary eyes and pain in her compressed lips. He bent down. "What happened? Who did this?"

She blinked and tears cascaded down her face, streaking her mascara and making her eyes look even bigger. "He—he was here." She sat up with a grimace.

"Don't move. You're hurt."

"He kicked me," she said, pressing a hand against her left side. "It hurt." More tears.

It was killing Ray that he couldn't pull her into his arms and comfort her. But he was FBI. She'd been assaulted, and his first obligation was as a law-enforcement official. He had to follow procedure. "I've got to call 911," he said, reaching for his phone.

Beside him, she pushed herself to her knees, then tried to stand, but she couldn't. She collapsed back to the floor.

"Molly, stay still. You might have a broken rib— Yes." He interrupted himself when the 911 operator answered. "This is Ray Storm, with the FBI." He quickly rattled off Molly's address, described what had happened and requested police and EMTs.

"I want to get up," Molly said, trying again to push herself to her feet.

"No." Ray bent down beside her again, forcing himself into the professional, detached yet concerned mode he used when dealing with crime victims. "Let's just stay until the police get here. They've got EMTs coming, too. We'll see how you are before you start running any marathons, okay?"

"I don't want to run a marathon," she said drily. "I just want to make sure my skirt is covering me decently. Oh—" she gasped as she tried to move. Her hand went to her left side again.

He clenched his fists. "Tell me what happened."

She relaxed into a seated position on the floor with her back against the bed. "Okay, fine. Although, I'll just have to repeat it again when the police get here." She went to take a deep breath and gasped again. "Oh, boy," she whispered.

"Breathe shallowly," he said. "Did you get a look at the man? You did say it was a man, right?"

She nodded. "He was—" She looked at him. "He was doughy."

Ray gaped at her. "What?" he asked. "Are you saying it was Acles?"

She gave a short laugh that turned into a wince. Breathing carefully, she said, "I wouldn't testify in court, but I'd say the man who attacked me fit your description to a T."

"Son of a bitch," Ray muttered. "That slimy snake."

"Oh—" Molly cried out, her hand flying to her mouth. "Oh, no."

"What? What is it?"

"He got—" her voice broke into a sob "—got into—the safe. He got the papers."

Ray stared at her. *Papers.* At that moment he heard sirens, suddenly loud and close. "Hang on a second," he said. "I'll be right back."

"Ray—don't—don't leave me."

"I'm not, hon," he said gently. "I'm just grabbing something." He picked up the piece of paper from the floor in the hall and glanced at it. It was a memo, signed by Martin Hennessey, with handwritten notes in the margin. He heard the patrol car's siren right outside. Then they cut off.

Quickly, ignoring the guilt engulfing him, he folded the sheet and stuck it into his pocket. Then he went back to Molly.

Within seconds, two uniformed officers were on the scene, along with two EMTs. The EMTs examined Molly and bandaged her ribs while Ray talked to the officers. Then, once the EMTs were done, the officers questioned Molly.

After Molly gave them all the information she had, Ray told them about the car he'd seen peeling away from the curb. He gave the officers Acles's name and his office address and described the decade-old domestic hatchback to them. "I'd be happy to view a vehicle lineup if you need me to," he told them.

It was over an hour before the police left. They promised Ray they'd do what they could, but Ray didn't hold out much hope.

"Looks like a simple B&E to me," the senior officer said, surveying the chaos in Molly's guest room. "Ms. Hennessey just happened to interrupt him."

"Really?" Ray said. "Did I mention that Ms. Hennessey is Martin Hennessey's sister? The candidate for governor? You don't think that might be relevant?"

The officer just shrugged, and Ray got the message. This report would go into a file and never be seen again. Unless something else happened to Molly.

ONCE THE EMTS HAD declared that Molly's ribs were slightly bruised, and the police were gone, Ray stood watch in the living room while Molly showered. She came out wrapped in the pink silk kimono he'd admired the day before. But this time she wore a pink-and-white floral nightgown under it. She no longer had mascara streaked around her eyes and down her face, but he could tell that she was still on the verge of tears.

He smiled at her. "How're you feeling?"

She nodded and shrugged. "Okay," she murmured, but then she shivered. "I was so scared," she said, wrapping her arms around herself. "Silly—" she started, but the word got swallowed up in a little sob.

"Come here," Ray said, holding out his arms. To his surprise, she glided into his embrace as if she'd done it dozens of times. He pulled her close, resting his cheek against her hair. "It's okay, you know," he whispered. "You're okay."

Molly felt tears building at the back of her throat in response to Ray's sweet words. She gave a little shrug, because if she said anything, she knew she'd start crying.

"Hey," Ray said. "I'm here, if you want me to be. Just tell me."

He was rubbing a palm up and down her back. It was the most soothing, comforting gesture she'd ever felt, and yet at the same time it stirred erotic memories of them making love. It had been eight years and she had never forgotten the feel of his hands on her. A small shiver ran through her.

"I'll tell you what," he said. "The EMTs left me a couple of mild tranquilizers, in case you have trouble falling asleep. Why don't you take one and lie down?"

She clutched at his shirt and closed her eyes. "Who did this? Who would— Do you still think it was Martin?" she muttered.

"What I think is that you shouldn't think tonight. Tonight is for you to calm down, to rest and to try to forget everything except that you're safe. There's time enough to think about what happened tomorrow." He pulled away and looked down at her. "I'm going to get a glass of water for you and you're going to take a tranquilizer."

She nodded, suddenly too tired to argue.

"Good," he said. "Now, you get in bed." He let go of her and directed her toward her bed.

She obediently followed his lead. When he reached over her shoulders to pull off the kimono, she let him, and when he turned back her bedspread and sheets, she got into the bed, moving carefully. As she relaxed back against the pillows, her bruised ribs protested.

"Be right back," Ray said. He turned on a small lamp on the nightstand, then turned out the overhead lights as he went out of the room.

Molly closed her eyes, but all she could see behind her lids was the faceless man, hitting and kicking her, so she kept them open. She shuddered, which sent a stabbing pain through her side.

"Here you go," Ray said, bringing a glass of water over to her bedside table. "Take this."

"Do you really think I need—"

"It's not going to hurt a thing," he assured her. "And I'm going to be here all night."

For some reason she thought that should worry her, but it didn't. The fact that he was going to be here, in her house, keeping her safe, made her feel better than any tranquilizer ever could. "Okay," she said, taking the tablet from him and swallowing it with the water.

"Good job," he said with a smile, setting the glass on the bedside table, then stepped back around the bed and over to the door. He put his hand on the light switch. "Try to relax and let the tranq work. You'll be asleep in no time. I'll be out in the living room." He flipped the switch and turned out the light.

Immediately the darkness closed in around Molly and she felt the man's hands again, his sour breath, his soft belly against her side as he pushed her down. Felt again the toe of his shoe as he kicked her. "Ray—" she gasped.

He reappeared instantly. "What is it, hon?"

"Don't leave me."

He didn't answer right away. She saw his head go down briefly, then back up. "I'll get a chair," he said.

"Lie down with me?" she asked. "I just—I just don't want to be alone. I'm just really scared right now."

He was silent. Oh, dear, she'd made a mistake. "It's okay if you don't want to," she said quickly. "A chair would be fine."

Without a word, he sat down on the bed, kicked off his shoes and lay on top of the covers next to her. She could feel his heat warming her. She slid a hand out from under the covers and grasped his.

"Is this okay?" she asked in a whisper as she intertwined her fingers with his.

"Sure," he muttered.

"Thank you," she said quietly. "For everything."

Chapter Five

Ray didn't sleep—not much anyway. He lay still, next to Molly, until he heard her breaths even out into the long, smooth breaths of relaxed sleep. He didn't want to let go of her hand, but his arm was beginning to cramp.

Carefully he extricated his hand from hers. She had fallen asleep on her back. Her lashes fanned her cheeks and her mouth was slightly open. Without compressed lips, pinched nostrils and fear dimming her usually bright eyes, she looked young and lovely, like the girl he'd known before Katrina.

The same question he'd asked himself earlier came back to him. What would have happened between them if there had been no storm? He hadn't seen her since that Saturday night when he'd talked her into giving him copies of the evidence that proved that Martin Hennessey was guilty of skimming LDAT grant moneys. If he had seen her Monday, he was sure she'd have oozed hatred and resentment. That was certainly her attitude the day before.

Watching her as she slept, Ray found himself unable to look away from her soft, beautiful face, the peachy glow of her skin, the delicate curve of her jawline and the luscious *amuse-bouche* of her earlobe. He was feeling things he hadn't felt in eight years, since the last time they'd made love, on their last night together.

Surprise changed to dismay as the truth dawned on him. He'd never gotten over her. She'd been young, and so had he. He'd been smart, too—smart enough to know that seducing Molly was wrong, but not smart enough to understand that she would hate herself a lot more than she hated him if he coaxed her into giving up her brother. He hadn't known it then, but he knew it now.

He'd seen it in her face the instant she'd looked into his eyes in the middle of Canal Street. She resented and hated him because he reminded her of what *she* had done.

He squeezed his eyes shut and shook his head. If he had it to do over again, knowing what he knew now, he wouldn't seduce her to get evidence against her brother—would he?

"Ray?"

The word whispered across his mind like the brush of a feather or a quiet, sweet breath. "Yeah, hon?" he whispered back. "How you doing?"

"Better."

"Do you want that other Xanax tablet?"

She yawned. "No," she said, her voice sounding amused. "I think I'm relaxed enough."

"Good. Want me to go away so you can sleep?"

She didn't answer.

He leaned up on one elbow. "Mols? Everything okay?"

"No," she said finally. "I don't want you to go away."

"Okay, then. Go back to sleep." He lay back down and stared at the ceiling, thinking it was going to be a long night. Because there was no way he'd sleep a wink with Molly there beside him in that filmy pink-and-white nightgown. He listened to her breathing even out again. Then he closed his eyes and tried to clear his mind, but it was stuck in a loop, replaying the sight of her crumpled on the floor during that split second before he saw that she was alive. During that instant, he'd felt as though his heart had been ripped from his chest.

"Ray?"

He opened his eyes and glanced sideways at her. "Yeah?"

"Could you hold me—just for a little while?"

He gritted his teeth. *No!* he wanted to say. How much willpower did she think he had?

"Yes," he said aloud. He could hold her, but it was going to be torture. For a moment, he lay there, at a loss as to what to do next. Did he get under the covers? Would she come out from under the covers? Either way, it didn't look good for his willpower.

"You should get under the covers," she said as if reading his mind. "You should take your jeans off. They're going to be uncomfortable."

No, I shouldn't, he thought, even as his hand went to the button and zipper at the front of the jeans. He got up, slipped the jeans off over his already growing arousal, then turned the cover down and climbed into the bed. "I'm not sure this is a good idea," he said as he tentatively reached out for her. He didn't want to get too close, so he hoped she'd be content with just his hand across her belly.

"Me, either," she said, laying her hand on top of his. "Ray, how did you get here at the exact right time?" she asked thoughtfully.

"I drove by to check on you, to be sure everything was all right."

Her fingers curled over his. "And how did you know it wasn't?"

He took a deep breath. "Your lights were on, but I didn't see you inside anywhere, and I—I just didn't like it. I had a funny feeling there was something wrong."

Molly propped herself up on one elbow and held his hand there, at her waist. "You rescued me," she said, then she leaned forward and gave him a kiss on the lips. It wasn't a long kiss. As kisses went, it was pretty chaste. But the feeling of her soft lips against his sent a surge of desire as strong as Katrina's floodwaters raging through him. He shook his hand free of hers, reached up to wrap his fingers around the back of her neck and kissed her. He held himself back, pressing his lips as gently, as chastely, against hers as she had against his.

She drew in a sharp breath that felt cool against his mouth. "Ray?" she breathed. It was a question, but he didn't know if it was directed at him or at herself.

"Mols," he muttered, then dived headfirst into her embrace. He kissed her fully now, openmouthed, tasting her with his tongue, flirting with hers and nipping at her lips.

She collapsed back onto her pillow, pulling him with her, and opened up to him in a way she hadn't known how to before. He felt guilt engulf him as he noticed and recognized all the differences between the girl he'd known eight years ago and the woman he was kissing now. There was an achingly sweet newness about a girl who had never made love before. A self-conscious, awkward eagerness that is completely lost after that first time.

But this woman, this Molly, turned him on in ways the girl never had—never could have. He pressed himself close to her, letting her feel how much he wanted her. She moaned, a knowing, yearning moan that encompassed a full understanding of what it was she craved.

He gazed down at her, seeking her true feelings in her eyes, but she closed them and reached for his mouth with hers.

A small gasp escaped her lips.

"You're hurt—" he started, pulling back.

"Shh," she whispered, "I'm fine." She moved his hand to her breast.

He caressed it, rubbing his thumb back and forth across her nipple. Her back arched, giving definition to all the exquisite curves and valleys and hills that made her body a woman's body. He kissed her more deeply, sliding his hand beneath her back and pressing her breasts into his chest.

"Hang on," he muttered. He held on to her and flipped over so that he was now lying on his back and she was atop him. "This'll make it easier for you to keep from hurting your ribs."

Faint surprise widened her eyes but lasted only a split second. She smiled languidly and bent down to take his earlobe between her teeth. The unexpected pleasure/pain combination slid across his nerve endings, spiraling quickly down his spine to his groin, where it caused his arousal to pulse with desire. He gasped and raised his head until he could delve his tongue into the soft, deep indentation at the center of her collarbone. He licked and sucked, then nibbled his way along the bone until he heard her breathing hitch and speed up.

She curved her back and tried to coax him to kiss her by planting little tongue kisses along his jawline and neck. Then she bit down on his earlobe again.

"Ah—Mols!" he cried, almost losing it. But a second later he was back in control and he trailed his tongue down the center of her chest until he was in the deep cleavage between her breasts.

He found her left nipple and suckled it until she moaned and begged him to stop. Then he turned to her right breast, sliding his tongue around and around, teasing at the dark pink edge of her areola, but not touching the nipple itself as he ground his arousal against her inner thighs. He stopped and looked at the swollen pink nub. He breathed on it, eliciting a gasp of delight from her. Then finally he took it into his mouth and sucked on it until he could feel it throbbing with reaction. He bared his teeth and grazed the tip, then bit down.

Molly couldn't stop the quiet scream that burst from her throat. Her back arched as his teeth scraped across the sensitized tip. She felt his arousal against her and felt herself contract in anticipation. "Ray," she moaned, "please." She put her palms against his chest, and his nipples pebbled against her skin. "Now!"

He lifted her, then lowered her slowly onto his arousal. She felt his hardness probing, sliding, filling her, inch by inch, until she finally sank down upon him and their bodies melded and fused and she couldn't for the life of her say where she ended and he began.

He'd barely begun to move inside her when her yearning swelled and grew to a fever pitch. Her heart was pounding so fast she could barely breathe. Somewhere in the recesses of her mind was a vague sense of soreness and pain in her side. But in the next second, any hint of pain was lost in pleasure as he thrust hard, filling her completely. What had been yearning and need exploded into a blissful crescendo of pleasure unlike anything she'd ever felt before.

The next thing she was aware of was Ray pulling her close with an arm behind her head, so that she could nestle in the curve of his shoulder. Before she could rouse herself enough to say anything, he was breathing quietly and evenly. Smiling, feeling more wrung out and satiated than she'd ever felt before, Molly splayed her fingers across his taut abdomen and drifted off to sleep.

RAY AWOKE TO THE SOUND of a phone ringing. By the time he opened his eyes, Molly was rushing out of the bathroom with a towel wrapped carelessly around her, her hair damp and tousled and her eyes still heavy with sleep. The sight of her aroused him and he wanted to pull her onto the bed and make love with her again.

But she went straight to her bedside table, searching for her phone. When she didn't find it, she grabbed her pink kimono off the floor. She let the towel drop and tossed the kimono around her with an unconscious grace that made him instantly hard, then she rushed from the room.

He heard her answer the phone. He got up and quickly pulled on his jeans. By the time he got to the bedroom door, there was panic in her voice.

"What? Oh, my God, when?"

He got to the kitchen in time to hear her say, "What do you mean, last night?" Her fist clenched at her side. "He's not in the hospital?" Her voice rose in pitch and volume.

"I'll be right there," she said through clenched teeth. "You tell him I'll be right there." She hung up and stood there, frowning at her phone's blank screen.

"Mols? What is it?"

"It's Martin. He had a heart attack—around midnight *last night*." She brandished her phone in a frustrated gesture. "That was Flan," she spat. "He let Martin leave the hospital."

"I'm sorry, hon," Ray said. "He's had other attacks?"

"No. He's never sick. I don't know what happened."

"And Flan?" he asked. "Is that his campaign manager?"

"Right. His name is Flannery Thrasher," she said sourly as she headed toward the bedroom. "They apparently were talking when Martin had the attack. Thrasher probably caused it."

"I'll drive you," he said.

She grabbed a dress from the closet and slid it over her head. "No. I don't want you around my brother. He knows who you are. Seeing you will upset him. I need to make sure he's okay. I'm going to try to get him to go back to the hospital."

She compressed her lips as she slipped her feet into low-heeled sandals. "I can't believe the hospital let Flan take him home. I'm next of kin. Why didn't they call me?" She started out of the bedroom, then turned back. "Could you please make sure the house is locked?"

Her sandals clicked on the hardwood floors as she left, slamming the front door behind her. Once she was gone, Ray dressed.

He took a long look at the guest bedroom, where files and papers, pens and notepads were scattered all over the floor. He'd talked with the police officers about the break-in and Molly's assault, but once they'd left, his entire focus had been on her.

Now he crouched and looked at the file folders that had been thrown onto the floor. There were the typical folders found in anyone's file cabinet. He saw one labeled Martin, but when he sifted through the papers near it, he found only a couple of photocopies of newspaper clippings that pertained to her brother. The thief must have taken the rest.

He sat back on his haunches and surveyed the room. Molly had said he got the papers. She'd meant the incriminating memos and notes she'd taken from the LDAT files eight years ago. That proved Martin was guilty of embezzlement. Ray cursed and ground his right fist into his left palm.

Without those papers, the amount of evidence Ray had wasn't enough even to convene a grand jury, much less indict Hennessey. Of the four most influential people on the LDAT, Hennessey was the only one who'd never had to pay for his crimes. Remy and Mack had taken down Barnaby and Barrow. Patrick Flay was presumed dead. But the man who'd masterminded the crimes was still free to lie and cheat and steal from the people of New Orleans. And within a few months, as governor, he'd have enough power to spread his corruption through the entire state of Louisiana.

Ray felt the despair and humiliation that had overwhelmed him as the FBI helicopter airlifted him out of the death and destruction of Hurricane Katrina.

But he would not fail the people of New Orleans this time. He would bring Hennessey down, even if it destroyed any chance he might have with Molly. And God knew he wanted another chance with her. Last night had proved that to him. He still wanted her, still desired her, still wondered what his life would be like if they'd met under different circumstances.

He scrubbed a palm across his face. He needed to focus on his next move if he was to have a prayer of stopping Molly's brother. When he opened his eyes again, he spotted the small fireproof safe sitting in the bottom of Molly's closet. The door was open and he could see from fifteen feet away that it was empty. The thief had obviously forced her to give him the combination.

Ray stood, and when he did, he caught a flash of sunlight reflecting off something. He walked over and picked it up. It was a ruby ring that had been left behind. He picked it up and stuck it in his pocket. When he did his fingers touched something—a folded sheet of paper.

With everything that had gone on last night and this morning, he'd forgotten about it. He pulled it out of his pocket, unfolding it as he walked over to the window.

As he looked closely at the printed words on the sheet and the handwritten notes in the margins, his hands began to shake. This was it! The most damning piece of evidence Molly had shown him all those years ago. This was the original memo that Molly had saved, because as loyal as she was to her brother, he was a thief and an embezzler, and she was too inherently honest to destroy the evidence of his crimes.

Ray let his gaze skim the incriminating margin notes written in purple ink in Martin Hennessey's precise, neat hand and thoroughly annotated and initialed as only an attorney would do.

That bumbling idiot Acles had dropped the most valuable thing he'd taken from Molly's house. The question was, had Molly had copies in the safe? Would whoever sent Acles to rough up Molly and steal the incriminating evidence against her brother think he had everything? Or would he believe Molly still had the most damning piece of evidence and come after her again?

Ray carefully refolded the sheet of paper and put it back into his pocket. He made sure Molly's house was locked, then he got into his rental car and headed for the Sixth District Police Station. He wasn't taking any chances. He had the proof he needed to take down Hennessey, or at least start a thorough and highly visible investigation into his practices as head of the Louisiana Disaster Avoidance Task Force. He wasn't going to wait another hour to turn the memo over to the local police and have charges filed against Martin Hennessey.

When he got there and told Detective Fortune he wanted to

file some evidence, the detective invited him to have a seat. "I've got some information for you," he said.

Ray wasn't sure he could sit, so he perched on the edge of Fortune's desk. But as soon as Teague started talking, he pulled up a side chair and sat.

Chapter Six

When Molly got to Martin's condo, he and Thrasher were in his bedroom, voices raised. She walked across the foyer and through the living room to the double doors to Martin's bedroom.

"Oh, hell, no. You can't do that to me!" Thrasher yelled. "I won't let you."

"Flan, I have to think of my health. My family," Martin said quietly, but Molly could hear the strain and fear in his voice. "I'm not going to let you make this decision for me."

"You're not going to *let* me?" Thrasher's voice rose in pitch and volume.

Molly shoved the doors open and stomped in. "What's going on?" she shouted over Thrasher as she marched straight to Martin's side and took his hand. "Martin, oh, my God. You look awful!"

Martin was propped up against pillows on his bed, wearing a pair of maroon satin pajamas and leather house slippers. Thrasher was pacing back and forth beside the bed, one hand pulling on his goatee.

She was shocked to see how gray her brother's complexion was. She'd seen him a few days ago and he'd been fine. He'd always seemed so big to her. At sixteen years her senior, he'd looked like a grown-up ever since she could remember. But now, he appeared small and frail—and old. He was only forty-two, but for the first time she saw gray hairs at his temples and mixed in with the dark brown.

Martin smiled faintly. "Thanks, Molly. You always flatter me. I guess I had a heart attack," he said, sounding as if he was having trouble getting enough breath to speak.

"I'm sorry," she said, kissing his forehead and noticing how clammy it felt. "Why aren't you still in the hospital?"

"It was mild," Thrasher said. "Nothing to worry about."

Molly shot Thrasher a withering glance. She wanted to tell him to get out of her brother's bedroom. Turning back to Martin, she asked, "What did the doctor say?"

"Well," Martin said, his hand squeezing hers, "the doctor seems to think it would be a good idea for me to have surgery—"

"That's ridiculous," Thrasher broke in. "You're as healthy as a horse. Bypass surgery is the latest trend. We'll give them a million to start a new cardiology wing and they'll change their minds."

"Flan," Molly cried in frustration, "shut up! Could you give us a minute? I'm trying to talk to my brother."

"Martin," Thrasher said, ignoring Molly, "we've got to go over your speech for the campaign kickoff dinner." He looked at his watch. "And in an hour, I'm holding a press conference at campaign headquarters."

"A press conference?" Martin repeated, sounding exhausted. "Why?"

"Because somebody at the hospital is going to leak that you were rushed there at midnight last night—if they haven't already."

Martin sighed and laid his head back against the pillows. "Could—could we have a few minutes, Flan?" he asked. "Then we can work on the speech."

"Oh, no," Molly said. "You're not working on anything. You're going to rest. In fact, you may be going back to the hospital, if I decide you need to."

Thrasher sent Molly a menacing look, and for an instant, the dark expression on his face seemed familiar. But before the thought fully formed in her brain, he turned and left, slamming the double doors behind him.

"Ugh," Molly said, making a face. "I don't know why you let him act like that. You know Jan can't stand him. If you'd get rid of him she'd come home. I know she would."

He sighed. "I'm tired, Molly. It was a long night."

She touched his forehead. "Why didn't Thrasher call me?"

"He— We didn't want to worry you."

"Marty, come on. I'm your sister." She gave him a small smile.

"Do we need to have the *Molly's a grown-up now* conversation? Again?"

His expression lightened a little.

"Okay." Molly reached for the bedside table phone. "If you don't tell me exactly what happened right now, I'm calling an ambulance and taking you back to the hospital."

Martin scowled at her. "Molly—"

"I mean it."

"Fine. Flan and I were having a discussion about—" he paused briefly "—about some specifics of campaign funding."

"You mean an argument," Molly interrupted.

Martin sighed. "Call it what you will. We disagreed and Flan started ranting," he said. "I was waiting for him to run out of air, but before he got winded, my chest started hurting."

Molly's heart skipped a beat. She couldn't imagine life without her brother. He was her only family.

"Flan brought me some ice water, but it got worse, so he drove me to the hospital."

"Well, thank God. I'm surprised he didn't try to argue the pain away."

Martin smiled. "He did, but I raised my voice."

Molly couldn't help but smile. "You raised your voice? Really?"

He shrugged. "I knew what was happening."

Her smile faded immediately. "What do you mean you knew?"

"I've had chest pains a few times before."

"Marty! Why didn't you tell me?"

"They were nothing serious."

Molly threw her hands up. "Oh for goodness' sake. Why didn't you stay in the hospital?"

He leaned his head back against the pillow, looking sheepish. "Flan was worried about the media."

"Flan was worried." Molly propped her hands on her hips and glared at her brother. "Do you know how much I care about what Flan thinks?"

"How could I not?"

She turned on her heel and stalked toward the double bedroom doors.

"Where are you going?" Martin called.

She held up a hand without turning around, then pulled the doors open. "I wanted to make sure Flan isn't out there."

Her brother shook his head as she sat down on the bed next to him and spoke in a low voice. "When you said that you and Flan disagreed about campaign funding, what did you mean?"

Martin's pale face turned paler. "Nothing important."

With a sigh, she took his hand. "Martin, I'm all grown up now. I need to know what's going on—and yes, I know something is. I want to ask you a question and I want you to promise me you'll tell me the truth." ·

"Molly—"

"Promise me. I'll call the ambulance. I swear I will."

Martin laid his head back on the pillows and closed his eyes. "I'll tell you the truth," he said. "God help me, I've lied to you and everybody else long enough."

His words frightened her, but she'd come too far now. She had to know. "Is Flannery Thrasher blackmailing you? Is that why he's always here? Why you always do what he says?" For a long time, Martin didn't answer. He didn't even move. She waited, her head bent over his hand, which she still held. After a moment, she realized his hand was shaking. Then she noticed that his whole body was shaking.

She looked up. His eyes were still closed, but tears were slipping out from under his lids and coursing down his cheeks. "Ah, Molly, I made so many bad decisions. I've done so many people so wrong—" He swallowed the last word on a sob.

"You always told me that everything would be okay if I'd just tell the truth."

"It all got so out of hand so fast. Patrick said it would be easy." His breath caught in a sob again and he coughed.

Molly reached for the glass on the bedside table and handed it to him. "Patrick? Did you say Patrick?"

Martin nodded his head and sniffed. She took the glass and

handed him some tissues from a box. "It was all Patrick's idea. And then, when it all fell apart, he betrayed us."

"Betrayed you? How?"

"It doesn't matter now. He's dead."

Molly thought about the expression she'd seen on Flannery Thrasher's face. "Martin, you didn't answer my question. Is Flannery Thrasher blackmailing you?"

Martin looked at her and she saw the answer in his face.

"Oh, my God, he is," she gasped.

Martin sighed heavily. "He just showed up at my door one day, about five years ago, talking about going into business together. He had a scheme for bilking people out of their homes, fixing them up on the cheap and reselling them. When I told him I didn't want any part of it, he started talking about the Disaster Avoidance Task Force. You know, the LDAT. Talking about how people would feel if they knew that I'd skimmed moneys that were supposed to go to reinforcing the levees. I was terrified. How could he know about that?"

Molly listened, stunned. What she'd told Ray had been true. Martin had changed after Katrina. It had made her feel less guilty about never coming forward with what she knew about the skimming of funds. But now the past was catching up to him.

"Oh, Martin, we've got to call the police. This can't go on. What do you know about Thrasher anyway? Where did he come from? Who is he?"

"I don't know. He just showed up with threats and demands."

"Does he remind you of someone?" she pushed.

Martin looked up at her. "What do you mean? Who?"

Molly couldn't get Thrasher's face out of her mind, nor the eerie sense of déjà vu she'd felt when he'd glanced at her sidelong. There had been something there—something about the eyes. "Do you know for sure that Patrick Flay is dead?"

Martin's eyes widened. "What?"

"Do you think Flan looks like him?"

"Like Patrick? No. I mean, I never thought about it, but—" Martin paused, frowning. "What are you trying to say? That Flan is Patrick? That's ridiculous. I mean—he's totally different. His hair's a different color. His nose is completely different. He's got a beard."

"All those things can be easily changed. Even the nose."

"I don't understand. Where is this coming from?"

Molly sighed. "I didn't want to upset you," she said, "especially now. But someone broke into my house last night."

Martin gasped.

"Are you all right?" Molly asked.

He held up a hand. "I'm okay. Just a little queasy. Why didn't you tell me?"

Molly waved that question away. "When I got home, the man was there, in my guest room. He knocked me down and forced me to give him the memos and financial reports."

"The memos and reports you found in the files." Martin nodded bleakly. "The ones you gave that FBI agent back before the storm."

"I'm sorry, Marty. I couldn't get rid of them. You know how I felt about what you were doing."

"And if it hadn't been for the hurricane, you'd have helped that FBI agent—" He paused.

"Ray Storm," Molly supplied.

"Storm, right. You'd have helped him put me in prison."

Molly felt tears stinging her eyes. She shook her head. "I never understood why you took the chance of ruining your life by embezzling federal grant funds."

Martin's eyes turned red and damp. "I told you, it just happened. It's so much money. You think you can just take a little bit. That you'll put it back. But then that money's gone and nobody notices, and you think they won't notice if just a little more is missing. Then it gets out of hand." He spread his hands. "I'm sorry, Molly—" He coughed again.

Molly looked at the glass, but it was empty. "I'll get you some water." She picked it up and took it into the bathroom, rinsed it out and filled it from the tap. When she turned the water off, she heard Martin's voice.

"Oh, God—"

She ran. "Martin! Are you—" The glass flew out of her hand

and shattered when it hit the floor as somebody grabbed her arm and jerked her sideways. Before she could recover, an arm came around her neck from behind and she was jerked backward against Flannery Thrasher's body. Instinctively, she grabbed at his forearm, but he was strong. Too strong.

She'd gotten a fleeting glimpse of him out of the corner of her eye as he'd grabbed her, and underneath the paralyzing fear she felt that eerie sense of déjà vu again. She tried to scream but his arm squeezed more tightly.

"Give me your phone," he growled.

"I don't—" she started.

"Give it to me or I'll *search* you for it, and you wouldn't like that."

She took it out of her pocket. "Here. What—" But she wasn't able to finish. Flan grabbed the phone with his other hand, then pushed her toward the bed, where Martin lay, frozen, staring in shock at his campaign manager.

"Sit on that chair by the bed," Flan ordered her, "and don't touch anything."

Molly did as she was told. Her mind was racing. "I don't know what you're doing, Flan, but—"

"Shut up!" he snapped. Stepping up to the bedside table, he picked up the portable phone's base and snatched it out of the wall, then tossed it on the floor. It landed with a jangle. Then he picked up Martin's cell phone from the table. He removed the cell phone's batteries, then threw them onto the floor.

Flan cleared his throat. "Good. Now, I'm sure you're wondering why I gathered you together here." He laughed at his joke, then leaned forward.

"We," he said, pointing at Martin, then Molly, then himself, "are going to win the governor's race, aren't we, Martin?"

Martin murmured what sounded like agreement. Molly wanted to yell at him, but she understood now. He couldn't go against Thrasher. Thrasher was blackmailing him.

"See, Molly?" Flan said, cutting his gaze over to Molly. "Martin and I are in perfect agreement."

"You're blackmailing him!" she cried. "What have you got on him that would make him go along with you?"

"You don't know? You should try to think harder, Molly."

Thrasher smiled and Molly saw again the familiar expression on his face, and this time her suspicions were realized. "You're Patrick Flay," she gasped.

Chapter Seven

Molly couldn't believe it had taken her this long to notice the similarity between Flannery Thrasher and Patrick Flay. "You're Patrick Flay," she said. "It's so obvious now. You lost weight, got your nose done, grew a beard, but it's you. You didn't die in Katrina." She sat forward on the edge of the chair.

"I told you to sit still and be quiet," Flan said. "We were talking about Martin being governor. We just need to be sure that everything goes smoothly between now and the election. And that's where you come in, Molly."

"Me?" she repeated, stunned. "I'm not going to help you—"

"Shut! Up!" Thrasher screamed. "I'm missing one piece of paper. It's the last scrap of evidence against your brother. I know you have it."

"Dear God, I see it now," Martin exclaimed. "Molly's right. You're Patrick Flay. You used the storm to disappear with— how much? You must have stashed away millions. Why come back? Why not just stay—wherever you were and enjoy all that money?"

Flan ignored his words. "Just think of the power. As Martin's sister, you can be first lady of Louisiana. I'll be secretary of state—the power behind the throne, if you will. Nobody will be able to touch us. I'll make sure of that."

"Why do you think we'd even consider this?" Molly said. "I'll go to the police. Better, I'll call the FBI."

"Oh, your little boyfriend. Right. I know he's back in town. Well, let me assure you that if you will *shut up* and let me finish, you'll understand perfectly. The reason we can all work together in harmony is very simple." Flan spread his hands and smiled. "I know where Benjamin goes to preschool and where Martin's wife, Jan, is. I know where they're living. Jan's sister has two beautiful little girls. You've seen them, haven't you, Molly?"

Molly's heart pounded in her ears. He was threatening Martin's family. Her family. "So, let's just get all the ugly details out of the way. Where is the memo?"

"I thought you got everything," she said. "It was all in the safe in my closet."

"Yes, well. My bungling employee will pay for his mistake. He missed the most important piece of evidence."

Molly swallowed hard. The man who'd attacked her had left something behind?

"Ah, you're thinking," Thrasher said. "Good." He pulled a bag from his pocket and tossed it to her. She caught it in midair.

"That's a prefilled syringe. It contains a large dose of an anesthetic. I want you to inject it into your brother's arm. In a couple of minutes, he'll fall sound asleep. While he's asleep, you and I are going to go get that memo. But be careful. If you accidentally hit a vein, you'll give him an overdose and he'll die. You're supposed to shoot it into the muscle."

She shook her head.

"If you don't, I'll use this." He pulled a second syringe out of his pocket. "It's potassium. It will stop his heart. And since he just had a heart attack last night, no one will question another, fatal attack today."

"Okay," she said.

"Molly—" Martin said.

"Don't worry," she responded, standing carefully and moving slowly over to her brother's bedside. "He's not going to kill us. He needs you to be governor." She sent Thrasher a disgusted look. "He can't do it himself."

"All you have to do is pinch the arm muscle, plunge the needle into the muscle, then press the plunger slowly."

She did what he'd told her. After about five seconds, Martin's eyes drifted shut. "That's it," she said. "I'm not giving him any more."

"No!" Thrasher cried. "Give him the rest."

She pulled the needle out of Martin's arm. "Make me," she

said, pointing it at Thrasher. Martin moaned but didn't wake completely.

"You stupid cow—" Thrasher started.

Just as he spoke, a huge crash sounded from the direction of the foyer, and suddenly there were hard, resounding footsteps and people shouting.

"Police! Freeze!"

"Get your hands up!"

Ray. Molly turned. As soon as she realized her mistake, she turned back toward Thrasher, but she was too late. He crossed the three feet that separated them, knocked the syringe out of her hand and grabbed her.

"No!" she screamed, struggling, but he managed to get her into a choke hold, just like before. Only, this time, she felt cold steel against her neck, just as she had when she was attacked in her house. She shuddered.

She stood as still as she could. "Please," she whispered, "let me go."

Thrasher moved the barrel of the gun from her neck to her temple. "Shut up!" he growled, just as Ray shouted, "Let her go, Flay! Drop the damn gun!"

Over their words was the deafening noise of heavy shoes and boots on hardwood as police officers entered the room.

"Drop the gun!"

"Flay. Put the damn gun on the floor and step away from Molly!"

Molly couldn't see the face of the man holding her—Thrasher or Flay or whoever he was—but she could feel his heart beating against her back and could hear his gasping breaths. He was panic-stricken, and she knew that didn't bode well for her.

"Flay, I'm giving you to the count of three to drop your weapon," Ray yelled. "One."

Molly looked into Ray's eyes, realizing that he was calling him Flay. He'd figured it out, she thought in relief. He knew that Thrasher was Flay.

"Two!" Ray yelled, raising his weapon and sighting down the barrel.

Don't shoot! The thought screamed through her mind. Martin was lying in the bed right behind Thrasher and her. *Don't kill my brother.*

As if he'd heard and understood her, Ray sidestepped until he'd passed in front of a police officer who held a handgun aimed at Thrasher. Molly followed him with her eyes. Watching Ray and seeing in his bearing and his expression that he knew exactly what he was doing was the only thing that kept her from panicking. She concentrated on staying as calm as she possibly could, hoping her lack of panic might influence Thrasher.

Ray kept his eye on Flay. That son of a bitch had fooled everybody, Molly included. And now he held Molly in a choke hold, and there was no way Ray could take him out without the risk of hitting her.

He didn't want the other officers to shoot, either. He hadn't wanted them here at all, but he'd lost that argument at the district station. He'd been forced to wait for backup, because that was what procedure called for. But it had rankled.

When he broke through the doors and saw Molly being held at gunpoint by Flay, he'd nearly lost it. Then, when she saw him, hope and trust filled her eyes. *Trust?* Did she really trust him? And did he deserve that much unwavering faith?

He looked at her now and tried to send her a message that everything was going to be all right as he continued moving sideways, then backward until he was standing next to the police officer in charge, Sergeant Drake Lane. "How 'bout calling off your officers, Sergeant?" he whispered to Lane. "I got this now."

"No way, Special Agent Storm," Lane responded quietly. "You don't got it."

Ray never let his weapon waver from Flay's right eye. "Flay's holding her too close. A shot will hit her."

"Our job to worry about, Mr. Storm."

"You're sure, Sergeant?"

"Yes, sir, I am."

"Okay, then," Ray said. He started toward Flay.

"Special Agent Storm!" Sergeant Lane snapped.

"No closer, Storm," Flay yelled at the same time. "I'll shoot her. I swear I will."

"This is not going to end well for you, Patrick" Ray said.

"Don't call me that. Patrick is dead. What the hell is this anyhow?" Flay asked. "You busted into a private residence."

Ray's vision went red. "I'll tell you why we *busted in*. You're wanted on numerous counts of fraud, specifically conspiracy to steal federal grant moneys from the state of Louisiana."

"I don't know what you're talking about. I wasn't even living here eight years ago. And wouldn't the statute of limitations have run out?"

Ray laughed. "Oh, come on, Flay. You're smarter than that. I never mentioned when the fraud was committed. And seriously, how can you claim you're not Flay and at the same time talk about statutes of limitations that apply to Flay. Besides—" Ray took a breath.

Molly spoke up. "There's no statute of limitations on a plea bargain, Thrasher, or Flay, I guess I should say."

"Shut up!" Flay yelled and Ray saw the gun's barrel sink deeper into the skin of Molly's temple. She winced. Ray's hand tightened on his handgun and his finger twitched—actually twitched—to pull the trigger. But he couldn't do that, any more than he could allow the police officers to pull theirs. Any gunfire in the room and Molly or her brother could be hurt—or killed.

"Flay, you've got two choices," Ray said. "You can drop the gun and go with the officers here, or you can shoot me." Slowly and deliberately, Ray bent his knees and set his handgun on the floor.

"Ray, no!" Molly cried, at the same time as Sergeant Lane spat, "Storm, what the hell are you doing?"

Ray ignored them and started walking toward Flay. He looked Molly in the eye and kept trying to send her his mental message.

She never took her eyes off him. Those bright brown eyes widened in fear and her mouth opened as if she wanted to scream at him to stop. He continued on, slowly, steadily.

"What the hell—" Flay cried. "Stop! I'll shoot you. Stop!" Flay took his gun away from Molly's neck and pointed it at Ray, which was exactly what Ray wanted him to do. He breathed an internal sigh of relief as he raised his hands, palms up.

"Go ahead, Flay. Shoot me. Make it worse for yourself."

"I'll do it," Flay shouted. "Don't think I won't."

Molly gasped as Flay's arm tightened around her throat. But Ray couldn't let his gaze waver from Flay's eyes, not for a millisecond.

Flay lifted the gun and aimed it at Ray's head, which was the other thing Ray had been counting on.

Carefully, Ray softened his knees and rolled up onto the balls of his feet as Flay's dark eyes flickered so slightly that no one but Ray could see it. Then he dived from a standstill, straight at Flay's feet.

Flay's gun fired twice before Ray slammed into his shins. Flay and Molly fell in a heap on top of Ray. He managed to grab Molly around the waist and roll, pulling her with him. Once he felt her body hit the floor, he shoved her with all his might, then whirled back around to face Flay, who was scrabbling for the gun he'd dropped.

Before Ray could grab him, the three police officers were on top of the man. Within what had to be no more than five seconds, they had Flay facedown and were fastening handcuffs on his wrists and calling for manacles for his ankles.

Ray pushed himself to his feet. For some reason his head was hurting.

"Ray!" Molly cried, scrambling up. "You're hurt!"

At that instant a hot, wet drop of something tickled his temple. He wiped at it and his hand came away streaked with blood. He sent Molly a chagrined smile. "Must be a scalp wound," he said ruefully, right before he collapsed.

Chapter Eight

The next morning, Ray knocked on Molly's door with a shaky hand. While he waited for her to answer, he stuck his hands in his pockets, then pulled them out. He thought about taking his jacket off, but he was carrying his weapon in his paddle holster, so it was probably not a good idea. Just about the time he'd decided he was going to tear the bandage off his forehead because the hot sun was making it itch, she opened the door.

Molly stood there with the pink kimono wrapped around her and a toy truck in her hand.

"Hi, Mols," he said with a little smile.

She frowned, more puzzled than angry. "Hi," she said, checking the closure of the kimono at her neck.

"How're you doing?" he asked awkwardly. He'd never felt as uncomfortable, as speechless, as downright stupid, as he did right now. He owed Molly an explanation—a bunch of explanations. There were others who'd offered to do the job for him. Martin was one. Teague Fortune was another—as if he'd let that good-looking Cajun within twenty miles of her.

The only person who apparently couldn't give her the explanation she deserved was him. He'd spent most of the night in the emergency room, until the E.R. doctor decided to believe him when he said he collapsed because he was dizzy and not because of any kind of concussion from the bullet that grazed his head.

Plus, according to the FBI, he'd been wounded in the line of duty, and they wanted him back in Washington—now. Didn't matter that he'd been on vacation and not on duty at all.

In fact, there was a helicopter waiting for him at the airport. Talk about déjà vu.

"I'm fine," Molly said, although she didn't look fine. Somehow, in the fray, she'd gotten a cut on her lip and a bruise on her cheek. Ray didn't know how it had happened, but he was afraid it had been when he'd slung her out of the way after he'd knocked her and Flay down.

"You?" she asked shortly.

"Good." He pointed at his head. "Scalp wound." Then he checked his shoes, and after assuring himself they were still there but could do nothing to help him, he looked up again. "Can I come in for a minute?"

She blushed. "I'm not dressed. I was just about to—get dressed."

He smiled. More déjà vu.

"Fine," she said, scowling as if reading his mind. "Come in—for a minute."

Inside, she stood resolutely in the foyer.

"Okay," he said, drawing in a deep breath. "There are a couple of things you ought to know."

"Okay," she echoed him. But she didn't move.

"The memo. I found it on the floor in the hall," he blurted. As he had the first time he'd faced her, four days ago, he figured he might as well get it over with. "I stuck it in my pocket and didn't tell anybody until yesterday afternoon."

She didn't respond, nor did she move.

"A detective found out that Patrick Flay had a Swiss bank account. With some major nudging by the FBI and the CIA, we found out that there was fifteen million dollars in the account and that Patrick Flay and his brother, Theodore, were the only ones who had access to the account."

"His brother?" Ray saw a spark in Molly's eyes for the first time.

He nodded. "Patrick Flay has been declared dead. His brother, Theodore, who lived in Ireland until 2007, when he came to the U.S., has confessed to working with Patrick to move the money from the U.S. to Switzerland. He also confessed that he took the name Flannery Thrasher in order to come to the U.S. and blackmail your brother into running for governor. Theodore was sure, with all that money, Martin's intelligence and charisma, and the information he'd gotten from Patrick during the time

Patrick was Martin's attorney, he could in effect run the state of Louisiana." Ray shrugged. "Apparently he was more ambitious than Patrick."

Molly looked dumbstruck. "Is all that really true?" she muttered. "It sounds preposterous."

Ray nodded. "Ha. I know. Myself, I don't understand people who get off on power, but as we in the good old U.S.A. know, politics is full of them."

"Does Martin know all this—"

Ray nodded. "I ran by the hospital earlier and filled him in. He feels terrible about not realizing who Thrasher was, but that's not his fault. Nobody knew, until that techie buddy of Fortune's dug up that Swiss account."

"Wow," she said, putting a hand to her forehead.

"Yeah."

Molly watched him, seeing how nervous he was and wondering what else he had to say to her. The way he was acting, Molly was pretty sure she knew what it was and she was real sure she wasn't going to like it.

But then, could she really expect anything else from him? When she'd known him before, he'd been all about his job. When he showed up again after eight years, it was because of his job. And now, she was certain, he was about to tell her that he had to leave—because of his job.

She took a deep breath. This time, she didn't want to be the one left with a broken heart. "Ray," she said.

"Mols—" he started in the same breath. Then, "Go ahead."

She nodded. "Look, I know you came back here to finish what you started eight years ago—"

To her chagrin if not her surprise, he nodded sagely.

"And you did. I'm thankful for what you did for Martin. If he actually can get probation for his part in the grant-money diversion, it will be like a new lease on life for him. He wants to keep up the philanthropic work he's been doing, once he recuperates from the bypass surgery the heart doctor told him he has to have. And Jan, his wife, has been with him in the hospital ever since yesterday. She spent the night there last night."

Molly smiled and held up the toy truck. "Benjamin stayed with me. Jan picked him up a little while ago."

"Martin has filled in a lot of the blanks for us, from back then and from now. He's been a big help in getting the goods on Theodore Flay."

"Thank you, Ray," Molly said, her expression softening. "I appreciate everything you've done." She leaned forward and kissed him on the cheek. "Everything," she whispered.

To her surprise, he wrapped his arms around her and pulled her close. "Everything?" he muttered.

"Ray," she said, putting as stern a tone into her voice as she could. "I don't want this."

"Then why'd you start it?"

"I didn't—" she faltered "—didn't mean to. I mean, it's over now, right? You're going back to Washington."

"Shut up and kiss me," he demanded, then covered her mouth with his.

She dropped the toy truck, and all the determination Molly possessed drained out of her at the feel of his lips. She tried—really hard—but she couldn't stop kissing him back. Then when he kicked the front door closed behind him and pushed the kimono off her shoulders, gasping when he saw that she was naked beneath it, she couldn't make herself stop him.

When he took her hand and led the way into her bedroom and laid her down on the bed, then stripped and lay beside her, she knew she was doomed. Because she didn't even want to stop him.

They made slow, tender love, each of them feasting on the other's body as if it were the first time all over again. Molly lay back against the pillows as Ray used his mouth to take her to complete and utter satiation, then she pushed him back against the sheets and did the same for him. Languidly, they continued to stroke and caress each other until they once again came together and made love until neither one of them could move.

When Molly opened her eyes, she found Ray watching her, a softness in his dark eyes she'd never seen before. She sat up and pulled a corner of the sheet over her. "I didn't mean to—" she started.

"I know, hon," he said softly. "But I did."

She started to get up, but he stayed her with a gentle touch on her arm.

"I need to get dressed," she protested. "I want to go see Martin in the hospital."

"You've got plenty of time," he said, still watching her.

She looked at him questioningly, and caught a subtle change in his face. He looked a little…scared.

"Ray. What is it? Is there something else you need to tell me?"

His gaze wavered for an instant, then he looked her in the eye. "Yes," he said solemnly. "It's not going to be easy to say this, because I know how you feel about me."

That surprised her. Did he? She'd thought she'd hidden the fact that she'd never gotten over him. She shook her head. "It's okay. Trust me. I'm fine. I understand perfectly. You don't have to—"

He put his fingers on her lips. "Mols, I have no earthly idea what you're talking about, but could you shut up for a minute and let me finish?"

If he only knew how badly she wished he would never finish. If talking would keep him from leaving, she'd talk until she wore her tongue out. But suddenly, she couldn't think of a thing to say, except *Don't go.* And she sure couldn't say that.

"Do you remember my telling you about Remy Comeaux and Mack Rivet?"

"Who?" The question surprised her. She knew the names, but her brain wasn't working very well right now.

"The two police officers who were on my investigative team back before Katrina."

"Oh, sure." Why was he dragging this out? She pulled on the sheet, trying to get more coverage. She didn't want to be naked when he left her.

"Well, they're opening a private investigations business, here in New Orleans."

"Ray, please!" she cried, crushing the cotton sheet in her fists. "I can't stand this. Please just go!"

"Go?" He looked genuinely shocked. "You want me to go?"

She uttered a small, frustrated scream. "No, I don't want you to go. But it's what you do. And I don't think I can stand this much longer. Could you just leave so I can start getting over you again?" Oh, no. She hadn't meant to say that.

Ray stared at her for a second, then started laughing. "Oh, Mols, hon. I'm making a huge mess of this. I don't want to go."

"You don't?"

He shook his head and became serious. "If you think you can forgive me and give me a chance to prove how much I love you, I'll quit the FBI today. I've got an open invitation to go into business with Mack and Remy."

"Forgive? Oh, Ray." A lump lodged in her throat and she couldn't speak. All she could do was reach for him as tears began to course down her face.

"Is that a yes?" he said, his mouth near her ear, and she was certain she heard a catch in his voice. She nodded and buried her face in the soft place between his neck and shoulder. After a moment, she managed to murmur, "I love you."

"What?" he said. "You what?"

She leaned back and swatted his arm. "I l-love you, you stupid man."

"Good," he said and pushed her down on the bed and moved above her. "I should be back in a week, after I've taken care of everything in Washington," he muttered between nibbles on her ear.

"Be back? You *are* leaving," she cried indignantly. "When?"

He kissed her long and hard, then lifted his head and smiled down at her. "As soon as I get to the airport, I guess." Then he kissed her again.

She turned her face away. "Ray? Stop it. As soon— Please tell me there's not a helicopter waiting for you."

He pressed his lips against hers. "There's a helicopter waiting for me," he whispered, tickling her lips.

"Ray," she said, trying to push herself up to a sitting position, despite the fact that his entire 190 pounds was on top of her. "You can't make them wait."

"Watch me," he said as he bent his head to kiss her again.

* * * * *

REQUEST YOUR FREE BOOKS!
2 FREE NOVELS PLUS 2 FREE GIFTS!

HARLEQUIN®

INTRIGUE®

BREATHTAKING ROMANTIC SUSPENSE

YES! Please send me 2 FREE Harlequin Intrigue® novels and my 2 FREE gifts (gifts are worth about $10). After receiving them, if I don't wish to receive any more books, I can return the shipping statement marked "cancel." If I don't cancel, I will receive 6 brand-new novels every month and be billed just $4.49 per book in the U.S. or $5.24 per book in Canada. That's a savings of at least 14% off the cover price! It's quite a bargain! Shipping and handling is just 50¢ per book in the U.S. and 75¢ per book in Canada.* I understand that accepting the 2 free books and gifts places me under no obligation to buy anything. I can always return a shipment and cancel at any time. Even if I never buy another book, the two free books and gifts are mine to keep forever.

182/382 HDN FVQV

Name   (PLEASE PRINT)

Address   Apt. #

City   State/Prov.   Zip/Postal Code

Signature (if under 18, a parent or guardian must sign)

Mail to the **Harlequin® Reader Service:**
IN U.S.A.: P.O. Box 1867, Buffalo, NY 14240-1867
IN CANADA: P.O. Box 609, Fort Erie, Ontario L2A 5X3
**Are you a subscriber to Harlequin Intrigue books
and want to receive the larger-print edition?
Call 1-800-873-8635 or visit www.ReaderService.com.**

* Terms and prices subject to change without notice. Prices do not include applicable taxes. Sales tax applicable in N.Y. Canadian residents will be charged applicable taxes. Offer not valid in Quebec. This offer is limited to one order per household. Not valid for current subscribers to Harlequin Intrigue books. All orders subject to credit approval. Credit or debit balances in a customer's account(s) may be offset by any other outstanding balance owed by or to the customer. Please allow 4 to 6 weeks for delivery. Offer available while quantities last.

Your Privacy—The Harlequin® Reader Service is committed to protecting your privacy. Our Privacy Policy is available online at www.ReaderService.com or upon request from the Harlequin Reader Service.

We make a portion of our mailing list available to reputable third parties that offer products we believe may interest you. If you prefer that we not exchange your name with third parties, or if you wish to clarify or modify your communication preferences, please visit us at www.ReaderService.com/consumerschoice or write to us at Harlequin Reader Service Preference Service, P.O. Box 9062, Buffalo, NY 14269. Include your complete name and address.

HI13

Colt saw that she had a stunned look on her face. Stunned and disappointed. It was heartbreaking.

Without a word, he took her in his arms. Hilde was trembling. He took her over to the couch, then went to her liquor cabinet and found some bourbon. He poured her a couple fingers worth.

"Drink this," he said.

"Aren't you afraid what I might do liquored up?" she asked sarcastically.

"Terrified," he said, and stood over her until she'd downed every drop. "You want to talk about it?" he asked, taking the empty glass from her and joining her on the couch.

She let out a laugh. "*I* hardly believe what happened. Why would I expect anyone else to?"

"I believe you. I believe everything you've told me."

Tears welled in her brown eyes. He drew her to him and kissed her, holding her tightly. "I'm sorry you had to go through this alone."

She nodded and wiped hastily at the tears as she drew back to look at him. "You're my only hope right now. We have to find out everything we can about this woman." And then she told him everything, from finding the shop vandalized to what led up to her being nearly arrested.

When she finished, he said, "We shouldn't be surprised."

"Surprised? I'm still in shock. To do something like that to yourself…"

"You knew Dee was sick."

Hilde nodded. "What will she do next? That's what worries me."

Colt didn't want to say it, but that's what worried him. "Maybe Hud has the right idea. Isn't there somewhere—"

"I'm not leaving. Dee told me that I've never had to fight for anything. Well, I'm fighting now. I'm bringing her down. One way or another."

"Hilde—"

"She has to be stopped."

"I agree. But we have to be careful. She's dangerous." He felt his phone vibrate, checked it and saw that his boss had sent him a text. "Hud wants to see me ASAP." Not good. "I don't want to leave you here alone."

"I'll be fine. Dee won this round. She won't do anything for a while and I'm not going to give her another chance to use me like she did today."

He heard the courage, as well as the determination, in her voice. Hilde was strong and, no matter what Dee had told her, she was a fighter.

Can Hilde and Colt stop Dee's deadly plan
before it's too late?

Find out what happens next in
CARDWELL RANCH TRESPASSER. Available March 19
from Harlequin Intrigue!

HIEXP0413BJ

It all starts with a kiss

Check out the brand-new series

HARLEQUIN KISS

Fun, flirty and sensual romances.
ON SALE JANUARY 22!